Malaysia Airlines Flight 370: The Perfect Crime

Colin Rousseaux

Dedication

This book is dedicated to those who are missing and to their loved ones and friends – the world is with you.

If you would like an eBook version of this novel, please visit www.stolen-mh370.com

Enquiries at info@stolen-mh370.com

For

Sophie, Max and Phoebe

Contents

Acknowledgments

I am indebted to my editor Tim Yaychuk for the many hours spent making this book what it is today. I also thank the following individuals for their critical input and I humbly thank them for spending time on a work in progress: Valerie Brown, Glennis Cohen, Nestor Hylnsky, Anne Gaylard, Stephen Goudy, Wanda Haschek, Paul Hempsey, Monique Larocque, Andre LaPointe, Kimberley Mansfield, Mario Nicoli, Maxime Rousseaux, Barbara Stevenson, Elena Shalaev, Jeff Smith, and Shengnan Zhang.

Cover design and proof reading by www.graphidome.com.

Photography courtesy of Natalia Kukleva

Join the discussion at www.stolen-mh370.com and maybe we can solve the mystery!

Preface

This book is a fictional account of the disappearance of Malaysia Airlines flight 370 in the early hours of March 8th, 2014. At the time of publication the airplane is still missing and so are the souls on board.

The characters represented in this tale are not based on real persons. However, the plot is built on publicly known events. I hope that the passengers on the real MH370 will be found someday soon safe and sound. Persons with friends and loved ones who boarded MH370 are cautioned against reading this book.

What follows is unadulterated fiction built around the scarce but widely known facts and filled with vivid imagination. Read on to find out more about the means, motive and opportunity for the theft of Malaysia Airlines flight 370.

The Means

Blood Diamonds

Diamonds are as portable as cash. More easily transported and hidden than any other form of capital, they are sought after when anonymity is required; their site of origin is almost impossible to identify. A cigarette package could easily hold a million dollars worth of diamonds and weigh only a few hundred grams. On the other hand, the gold standard would weigh over 140 kilograms and be worth half as much. One million dollars in one hundred dollar bills would weigh approximately 10 kilograms and be one meter in height.

Rebels in Angola, Sierra Leone, and the Democratic Republic of Congo frequently use diamonds as illegal currency to purchase weapons, giving rise to the term "blood diamond." The Kimberley process was developed in order to track diamonds and to prevent their use in financing of violence by rebel movements. The Kimberley process improved the situation but has failed to fully stem the flow of blood diamonds due to corruption.

Angola, located on the west coast of Africa is now the world's fourth largest diamond producer. It gained independence from Portugal on November 11, 1975. Although independent, the Popular Movement for the Liberation of Angola (MPLA), the National Union for the Total Independence of Angola (UNITA), and the

National Liberation Front of Angola (FNLA) fought in a civil war from 1974 to 2001. Between 1992 and 1998, UNITA sold blood diamonds, valued at 3.72 billion United States dollars, to finance its war with the government. UNITA leader Jonas Savimbi had in place the world's largest diamond smuggling network, netting hundreds of millions of dollars per year with which he bought arms and supported his own wealth. Despite a United Nations resolution, UNITA was able to continue to sell or trade diamonds in order to finance its war effort. It has been estimated that as much as 20 percent of the total production of diamonds in the 1980's was sold for illegal purposes and 19 percent were blood diamonds.

New members of the billionaire's club were created. Their newfound wealth could be used in any manner.

We must know what caused that airplane to disappear. – Sir Tim Clark, CEO, Emirates

Origins

Ming Gao's Lifetime Achievement Award

11:00: September 3rd 2013 – Beijing China

The deafening applause made 67-year old Ming Gao, professor emeritus at the Peking University School of Mathematical Sciences in Beijing, look down with embarrassment. Inwardly he was delighted to have received the lifetime achievement award for his work in mathematics. His Fu Manchu beard quivered with emotion as he relived times underlying the accolades bestowed upon him. The applause faded.

He looked into the crowd then removed a script from his suit breast pocket. "Thank you all for this honour," he began speaking in English with a hint of an Oxford accent he had attained while working on his PhD. The audience hung on his every word. Ming then went on to give a synopsis of the life he led. With just the right amount of humour and thanking all the appropriate persons he finished by saying, "None of this would ever have been possible if it were not for the unwavering support of my beautiful wife Bao-Yu. Thank you very much."

As he left, Bao-Yu beamed oozing pride from every pore of her body for this wonderful man she had by her side. His short thin silhouette walked towards her, his wise smile flowered as he walked into the light of the auditorium. His efforts to reach his beloved were thwarted by colleagues and newly minted graduates. They had come to see the great master that mathematically had defined fractals. He waved to Bao-Yu. His wedding ring glinted in the light.

The auditorium emptied. Ming politely excused himself from the groupies to see Bao-Yu. Rivulets of joy ran down her cheeks as she grabbed him in a hug that seemed to last forever.

Bao-Yu was flushed with excitement and short of breath. "Let's go home and relive our past. Lao gong I love you more and more each day." Ming remembered when they met in 1968.

"Me too." He pointed to the door. "We have to meet the dignitaries at the reception now Lao po, but we shall go home as soon as possible."

Bao-Yu held his arm tight. "It's such a pity that Li-Na could not come tonight. Melbourne is such a long way away."

Having returned home for a rest and to have tea they sat hand in hand on the sofa under the pictures of Li-Na at various times of her childhood and as a mother with young Li-Li.

They spent the rest of the evening walking down memory lane. They remembered the loss of his very strict parents who owned land and 'disappeared' during the Cultural Revolution. They remembered how the Red Guard misled them at the time.

Ming was a gentle person with an old soul. He was in touch with his inner child. He certainly deserved the lifetime achievement award.

Manny's Milk Bar and the Liu Family

07:30: March 4th 2014 – Melbourne Australia

Fond memories of a Milk Bar are part of life for anyone who grew up in Melbourne. George Staples remembered those days fondly. "When we were short of money we'd hunt for bottles and bring 'em back to Manny's. Sixpence a bottle! Hey presto, more sweets than you could eat!"

The Milk Bar was more than a shop. It was church for the regulars. Nowadays, coffee shops and convenience stores have sprung up to take their place. Competition from big business starves those that remain. Since the '90s the local Milk Bar has become a relic of yesteryear except for Manny's Milk Bar; a convenience store from the '60s.

Born Manchu Long Liu some 34 years ago, Manny with a Marlboro hanging from his bottom lip, had been up since five o'clock in the morning. He would have his second cigarette when he closed the shop. He brought in the bread and paper deliveries, opened the till and turned on the lights. A tram rattled by. By six o'clock he had two customers; each bought the morning paper. He looked at the peeling paint and remembered when he and his father last painted the shop. He was seven.

Manny was bored. Nine o'clock in the evening seemed far away. With great effort he resisted the urge to roll back into the arms of his bed just a few metres away upstairs. Even so, Manny, slight and obviously of Asian descent, considered himself lucky to live the life he does. His wife who he loves as much as when they were first married, Li-Na, his seven-year-old daughter Li-Li, and his mother, Jiao Liu, all live under one roof above the Milk Bar.

Trustworthy Li-Na came gracefully downstairs. "G'day darling. Slept well?"

Manny pushed her black straight hair out of her eyes. Li-Na gave him a big hug and then rested her head on his chest. She pulled back, smiled into his eyes, turned and called upstairs. "Li-Li it's time to get ready for school!"

No answer.

Manny cupped his hands as a megaphone. "Li-Li! You finished your homework last night, didn't you? Are you dressed yet angel?"

Li-Li stamped on the floor and dust fluttered down from the old ceiling. "I'm coming!" She didn't say when.

She appeared in her uniform and with a disarming smile ran to Manny's arms. "I love you dad." She gave him a big sloppy kiss. Manny melted and ruffled her hair, picked her up, threw her into the air and gave her a big 'daddy hug'.

He put her down and patted her on the head. "I love you lots and lots angel." She looked up at him with loving eyes.

Manny handed Li-Na a list. "I need you to order chips and soft drinks today."

"Of course I shall dearest when I get back." She left through the back door with Li-Li in tow.

The 1997 blue Mitsubishi Magna TE, semi-comatose, coughed to life filling the neighbourhood with blue smoke and sounding like a bag of hammers in an iron foundry. At 327,000 kilometres it was well past its expiry date.

Usually, Li-Li would have taken the seven thirty bus but today she missed it. Manny yelled above the cacophony of the geriatric machine. "Don't forget to pick up the Indian dishes on your way back!" He looked back at the backyard disparagingly noting the overfull dumpster, closed the gate and started back to the front entrance.

He looked at the cigarette butts on the pavement in front of the store; he would deal with them later. He opened the squeaky warped door and entered the Milk Bar. The door closed lessening the rumble of the morning rush hour traffic. It hit the suspended bell just before it shut.

The bell tinkled and the creaky door let in a familiar face. Manny looked up. His face lit up with a grin. "G'day Flo!"

Flo opened her fuchsia purse and took out a tissue. "G'day dearie." She hardly moved her lips then blew her nose smudging her lipstick.

"All righty then. Nice blue rinse Flo." Florence Banks was the local eccentric gossip. She draped her tall Rubenesque form with a homemade Sanderson style print dress, covered her face with wasp like glasses and wore way too much makeup. Flo had retired from teaching kindergarten four years ago and Manny's Milk Bar had become an extension of her home. She had known Manny's grandparents; the first Liu's to work and buy the Milk Bar and remembered them fondly.

George Staples pushed his 50-year-old beer belly through the door. His midriff knocked cans of mushroom soup off the shelves. "G'day Manny, how's it going mate?"

Flo chatted with George in front of the till. Manny was frustrated with their banter. "Flo. I made a cuppa tea ten minutes ago. Go and pour some for yourselves – over there! You're blocking my customers!"

Li-Na came in overflowing with Styrofoam containers wafting Indian aromatic scents. "The car needed a litre of oil – I think it's dying. She put down the containers and took out Manny's list. She walked around the shelves and added a couple of items.

Flo looked over the rim of her teacup. "How's Li-Li doing at school, dearie?"

"Very well and she still practices her violin." Li-Na's accent betrayed her 'new Australian' status.

The rest of the day seemed like any other at the Milk Bar – the same routine.

It was six o'clock when Manny looked upstairs. "Li-Na darling. Don't forget you're supposed to phone your parents."

"Okay. I was just going to do that now." Her voice trailed off as she started to dial Beijing.

The regulars had left: Flo for her Country Women's Association meeting and George to the pub to play darts.

Li-Na' was on the phone. Her voice was abnormally animated. Manny couldn't make out what she was saying. When he heard muffled sobs he ran up the stairs two at a time to find Li-Na crying with her hands held to her forehead. He hugged her against his peaceful soul.

Manny lifted her head. "What happened?"

Li-Na wiped her tears and her voice was shaky. "Baba told me that they had to take mama to the hospital." She shook and cried. "She couldn't breathe. Baba thought that she had a cold, but they found out why." She looked at the floor. "She has a heart problem and she's going to die." Li-Na exploded into tears. Manny's mouth dropped open.

Manny sat silent for a few seconds waiting until she recovered. "How's your dad doing?" Manny thought of the old professor. Ming must know what was coming. He knew a lot.

Li-Li had finished her homework and violin practice. "Let's go angel; it's time to get ready for bed."

Manny heard the tinkle of the door and slipped downstairs. "You go take care of Li-Li and let me know when she is ready for a story."

"We're ready!" Li-Li got out her favourite Blinky Bill book. She looked at the kangaroos fleeing an approaching bushfire. She sat on the couch being careful to avoid the spring that poked through the faded worn cover. Manny climbed the stairs dragging his feet.

Just before closing the bell tinkled again. "Uh." Manny closed the book and grunted as he got off the bed and realised that he needed more exercise. "Li-Li. Good night sleep tight mind the fleas don't bite, if they do pinch them tight then they won't another night." Her voice trailed downstairs to the customer below.

The little voice called after him. "You're the bestest dad in the whole world!" He stopped looked upstairs and smiled: a smile of paternal love.

Manny's Milk Bar was now closed. He cleaned up and swept the floors, bolted the door, pulled down the roller grid and locked it in place. He turned out the lights and went upstairs. Li-Li was sleeping – a flawless diamond. He bent down and gently kissed her forehead. She smiled in her sleep and turned over. Manny had a shower and joined Li-Na in bed. He lightly touched her arm. She rolled towards him. Tired though he was he fell into her arms.

Li-Na's Dilemma

Manny walked sleepily downstairs. He turned on the lights and prepared the Milk Bar for another day's business. Li-Na could not sleep. She had been talking to her father in Beijing every two hours or so during the night. She called down to Manny. Manny mounted the stairs and stood in the doorway to the living room. "What's the matter darling?"

"Baba says that the doctors cannot do anything more. Her heart is getting weaker."

He rushed to comfort her but sat carelessly on the couch and endured the spring's assault on his backside. "How long's she got?"

"She could die at any time."

The Ticket

Manny made the travel arrangements. At such short notice they managed to get two seats for MH128 leaving Tullamarine [MEL] just before midnight on March 6th arriving at Kuala Lumpur International Airport [KUL] at 06:40 in the morning on March 7th. The two would then have to wait nearly 18 hours in the airport until boarding MH370 just after midnight on March 8th, touching down in Beijing China at 06:30 local time on the same day. By the time that they cleared customs it would still be time for breakfast.

Ming phoned in the early afternoon and Manny answered. Ming announced that Bao-Yu had died and asked Manny to tell Li-Na.

Li-Na picked up Li-Li from school and entered the Milk Bar. When Li-Na saw Manny's face – she knew – her hand opened. The bag of bottled mango chutney dropped on the tile floor shattering her hopes with shards of mango-tainted glass. Li-Li started crying. Flo raced over to pick her up: "Come on dearie!" Instead she ran to Manny and jumped into his arms. "Dad! Why's mum crying?"

"Your grandmamma in China has just died. Remember mum and I talking about grand mama's heart?" Li-Li nodded and looked lovingly into Manny's eyes. He hugged Li-Li firmly trying unsuccessfully to hold back his tears. "It stopped."

"Oh. Did it hurt?" Li-Li fiddled with a bag of chips on the shelf next to her.

"No. She died in her sleep so it wouldn't have hurt. I'm going to make sure that you and mum get to the funeral. You can watch TV after homework tonight."

"All righty then!" Li-Li ran up the stairs.

Li-Na sat at the table with her head in her hands crying. Manny touched her on the shoulder and gently put his arm around her. "Li-Na. You must call baba right away."

Li-Na gained composure and climbed the stairs. The door was closed, but the anguish flowed down the stairs drowning the talk below. Manny went upstairs and found Li-Na as white as new snow. He held her hand. It was ice cold. "All righty then. Darling, you've got to get ready because I have booked a taxi for eight o'clock tonight. You will be with your family in less than two days!" He went through their itinerary with her.

Apart from his visit to China to teach English as a second language Manny had not been out of Melbourne or the Milk Bar. He was born in the Milk Bar. He grew up in the Milk Bar. He will probably die in the Milk Bar. He had not been without his girls for anymore than an afternoon and thought they would be safe.

He was mistaken.

The Motive - Greed

Echoes from the Past

Otto von Eschen came from humble beginnings. He was born the only child of Gertrude and Herman von Eschen in Munich during the twilight of the Second World War. His abusive father, who served in the Luftwaffe, took the opportunity to immigrate to German South West Africa before it became independent Namibia, to manage the tree plantations around Otjiwarongo. Otto attended secondary school in Okahandja and was top of the class. In 1962 he returned to Germany to take a bachelor of engineering degree at the university of Bremen. Upon his return he was employed as a mechanical engineer for the port of Walvis Bay (Namibian Port Authority). He found his employment boring and the wages did not buy much excitement. He needed something more.

The programmed stereo provided a precisely timed blast of Wagner's Tristan und Isolde. He woke from his foetal position and stretched and unfolded himself like a tortured paperclip and then rubbed his left knee. It was most painful in the morning but a hot bath, even in the summer heat always seemed to help. He slowly reached for the box of Gauloises cigarettes on his night table and took out the last one. Only sparks came from the lighter; he snarled and threw the defunct unit across the room. He perched his horn-

17

rimmed glasses on his eagle-like crooked nose to find a lighter that worked.

Now dragging on a lit cigarette, he inhaled deeply and moved stiffly to the bathroom. A tobacco haze followed him. "Scheisse!" Sparkle, the African grey parrot, had just completed his wake-up routine. Hunchbacked, skinny, short and pale, Otto was looking and feeling older than his age of nearly sixty. His pale blue sinister eyes came alive. He opened the faucets and shaved with a cutthroat razor while the water ran. He savoured the bath and relaxed.

His unassuming modern three-bedroom house in Klein Windhoek was perched on the side of the hill two blocks away from Am Weinberg restaurant looking south toward Keetmanshoop. It was sterile. Outside the sparkling pool beckoned phantom visitors. In the living room, tiles were alternate black and white in the shape of a chessboard for the proportionally sized army waiting patiently. Often he played against himself listening to his beloved Wagner, as Otto did not care for other music. Even his beloved Wagner and chess, which satisfied the complexity of his mind, did not satisfy his soul. It just delayed the emptiness inside. He was alone and lonely.

He sat in the bath soaking and smoking, holding his cigarette between his two remaining fingers on his left hand. He looked at his absent digits and remembered the event that occurred when he was young. He was working during his summer holidays at Windhoek Joinery Work on Gold Street in Prosoerita. The router slipped while he finished a moulding. His angelic fingers took flight to the other side of the room landing rather unceremoniously in a pile of sawdust. Blood from the router formed a line around the walls. He was left with his left ring and pinkie fingers at the age of 13. This only added to the abuse from his father.

The cuckoo clock, handmade in Bavaria and brought to Namibia when his family emigrated from Munich chimed 08:00. Katrina, punctual as usual, drove into the driveway in her old moribund Datsun wheezing a cloud of blue smoke matching the plume emitted from his lips.

Katrina entered the house. "Good morning sir."

Otto did not respond.

"Breakfast in half an hour!" Otto's stomach grumbled before he was conscious of the thought, a thought interrupted by the telephone.

"Did you want me to answer the phone, sir? "

"Ja!" He twisted his mouth exposing his teeth in a silent snarl. He always liked being called 'Sir' as he believed that such a salutation should be obvious. He could not hear the conversation, but the tone of Katrina's voice declared it was not a social call.

"Here is your message sir." She handed the note to Otto. "Can I get anything else for you sir?"

Otto did not look up. "Nein." Katrina headed off to the back of the house to start cleaning.

He walked to the second bedroom down the hall, which was now his office. He looked at the message: Babs Angula wants a meeting. He sat down in his ergonomic chair, turned on his computer and the banker's lamp. A rug partially covered the white tiled floor, which supported walls of books. There was no room for pictures and the window never stood a chance. "Babs, funny to hear from him again. It has been 27 years." He reached into his shirt pocket and removed a polished American silver dollar coin. He flipped it while he mused.

He stepped outside onto the porch, flipped his coin and opened a new box of cigarettes. With shaky hands he took a cigarette, lit it and admired the view. Windhoek is the Namibian capital. It rarely rains. He has always loved this place. It was in his blood. It was in his soul.

What did Babs want?

Child Soldier

It started years ago in Rundu on the Angolan-Namibia border when 15-year-old Babs Angula was supposed to be on his way home from school. It was an ordinary day. He did not excel at school but was the most popular student in his class. Like any other child he did good and bad deeds. It was 1975.

The Angolan Civil War (1975 – 2002) began immediately after Angola became independent from Portugal. A power struggle between two former liberation movements, the People's Movement for the Liberation of Angola (MPLA) and the National Union for the Total Independence of Angola (UNITA) degenerated into war.

The MPLA and UNITA had different roots in the Angolan social fabric. They were mutually exclusive despite their shared aim of ending colonial occupation. Politically, they posed as Marxist–Leninist and anti-communist forces. Two other movements, the National Front for the Liberation of Angola (FNLA) and Front for the Liberation of the Enclave of Cabinda (FLEC) complicated matters further.

The war became a Cold War struggle. Both the Soviet Union and the United States, along with their respective allies, provided significant military assistance to the parties in the conflict.

Furthermore, the Angolan conflict became entangled with the Second Congo War in the neighbouring Democratic Republic of the Congo (1998-2003) and the Namibian War of Independence (1966-1990).

A UNITA patrol ambushed Babs on his way to meet friends at the edge of the upper Zambezi River. They tried to take him but he escaped. When they started to shoot he stopped running and surrendered. Babs' life would never be the same.

He was beaten unconscious and sent to Luso in Angola to become a child soldier trained to hate and do repugnant things. Sleep deprivation, lashings, indoctrination and appalling living conditions changed him. With a gun in his hand and fuelled with drugs, he slipped over to the dark side. The innocence of the child had been annihilated.

He was now part of the Angolan civil war and was enjoying it. He was good at it. He became a sixteen-year old commander with his own youths to indoctrinate. He hated killing at first but then he began to like it. Later he enjoyed watching the rivulets of his enemy's life run into the sand. His stature and killing skills won him rapid promotion – and a command in UNITA.

The youthful Babs now commanded thousands of men, most of whom he had never seen. He reported to Jonas Savimbi. Most of these thousands were no more than a militia to

Babs: cutthroats and trigger-happy faceless creatures who obeyed his orders.

He was well educated and still played the piano. He took great pleasure in playing the second movement of Beethoven's seventh symphony to the condemned when led off for execution.

But that was yesteryear. Now he is retired General Babs Angula. Retired from the army that is, but not business. Babs had become insanely wealthy in blood diamonds, some of which were used to purchase weapons for the war effort.

His physique, voice and mannerisms commanded respect and still do. He was a young tall massive man with well-proportioned face, India ink skin, blood shot red eyes and perfect teeth. A scar on his left cheek accentuated his Cheshire cat grin. His unique booming laugh must be heard to fully comprehend its timbre.

In the early days this 16-year-old warlord had to move diamonds in exchange for cash for the war effort. Arms were bought. The excess remained in his pockets. His pockets grew and so did his greed. Babs wanted to crystallise his wealth. He was given the name of Otto von Eschen in Windhoek, Namibia as a reliable secretive diamond cutter and merchant to solve his problem.

Babs never trusted anybody unless he met them in person. He had not met Otto.

Otto had been called.

Civil War

12:00: October 29th 1976 – Cuanavale Angola

Joe's Beerhouse is where Otto ate his ritual Sunday gemsbok. The Oryx was his favourite meat. He had left his Boer hat on the table to reserve his place while he emptied the three pints of Windhoek Lager he had consumed in the previous hour. Relieved, he returned to find a folded note in the brim of his hat.

The script was handwritten.

Babs Angula wishes to meet you for a business proposition regarding "special stones." If you are interested, go to the Kalahari Sands and sit at the main bar. A girl will approach you and you ask her whether it will rain today. The correct response should be 'not in Windhoek, but in Luanda in the afternoon.' Then give her this note. Mr Angula will contact you by fax.

Otto supplemented his engineer's salary with a small diamond cutting business. He had learned the trade from an 84-year old German and recently bought his one-man business. Intrigued, he drove to the Kalahari Sands and sat down at the bar. Seemingly from nowhere a stunning young Herero lady in her twenties with a perfect hourglass silhouette came and sat down next to him.

She touched his arm. "How are you today, sir?" She smiled with picture perfect white teeth.

"I am very well, thank you. It smells like rain.

It will rain this morning don't you think?" Otto's high-pitched grating voice gave the doll goose bumps in the 35 degrees Centigrade weather.

"Not in Windhoek but I believe it will rain this afternoon in Luanda." Otto gave her the note and left.

He listened to the news as he drove home. *"In Angola today, the Union for the Total Independence of Angola, known as UNITA attacked many people from the People's Movement for the Liberation of Angola referred to by many as MLPA. Corpses were strewn everywhere but missing ears. A young Babs Angula led the skirmish. They took no prisoners.*

Also in the news today…" He turned off the radio and shook his head. He arrived at his home, pressed the remote and opened the double garage door. He parked on the left side, the right containing a 1950 VW Beetle, a restoration project never to be completed.

He bounced into the house, turned on Wagner and reached for the Schnapps bottle. Time to celebrate! He set about working on his hobby: model World War II aeroplanes. The aeroplane room had numerous model aircraft occupying all surfaces and suspended from the ceiling by fishing line. Paradoxically he hated flying due to motion sickness. He picked up a half completed model of the Avro Lancaster and opened the glue – the smell of the solvents brought glazed eyes and a quasi-smile.

The fax machine rang.

Otto was half pickled by then.

The machine ejected instructions for Otto to go to the Windhoek Eros Airport where he would fly to meet Babs. He was to be escorted by Elspeth, one of Babs' confidants in Windhoek to a private aeroplane tomorrow.

Otto finished his five kilometre daily run, showered and waited for his escort. An unassuming white Volkswagen Chico pulled up at the curb promptly at 15:00 and honked. Elspeth smiled at Otto as he climbed in. She was a buxom lady with a large posterior perfectly aligned with the term 'broad."

"Mr von Eschen. I'm to take you to the airport."

They entered the airport building and once they cleared security she led Otto to a hangar where a four-seat Piper and three men were waiting. Two were dressed in fatigues and the other was dressed as a civilian. He stopped and looked around. The men were between him and the aeroplane. Elspeth had left the hangar. Suddenly Babs' trusted lieutenant Charles Mutorwa gripped Otto's arms tightly while the other man in fatigues patted him down. He tried not to panic.

"Okay. Babs just wanted to be sure." He released his grip. "Up you go."

Otto sprung into the co-pilot's seat and put on his harness. The men in fatigues got in the back.

He realised that this was no normal commute and there was no way out. It was now 15:39.

Charles Mutorwa had a blue cloth bag in his hand. "We have to blindfold you until we get there." This was an order, not a request. Otto was claustrophobic and this was not what he had planned for. The cloth bag was soft but he could breathe.

Blindfolded and trying not to hyperventilate, Otto listened to the engine turn over, cough, then start. The Piper took off, climbed and headed north. Time ticked by. Nobody said a word. Eventually the bag was removed. All he could see in all directions was thick verdant vegetation poorly illuminated by the setting sun. The pilot was a 24-year-old good looking Angolan of average build with fine bone structure. His head full of curly dark hair and smiling brown eyes were totally disarming – fatal for women.

"Flavio's my name, flying's the game. Good to meet you! Crazy flyin' out here but the cash is good!" Flavio Ribas was known as a cowboy behind the yoke of an aeroplane. His trophy shelf attested to his acrobatic abilities. The conversation was one sided as Flavio proceeded to regale Otto with stories about the missions he had flown.

The Piper droned on over the mounds of vegetation and life below. The men in the back did not talk. Otto held his stomach and groaned.

Flavio mumbled to himself in Portuguese and then turned to Otto. "I hope your stomach's made for this shit!" He signalled Otto to look at the ground. Otto did not want to but did so in his rare submissive state. He turned pale and his muscles tightened. He bit his lip and started to shake uncontrollably holding his stomach.

A small clearing could be seen not far ahead amidst almost impenetrable greenery. The inside of the small aircraft seemed to close in on him. His claustrophobia squeezed him like a python. He wiped his brow and tried to think of diamonds. This did not help.

"There's our landing strip." Flavio pointed out a scar in the verdant scene. "Hold on tight! Far too many pissed off soldiers still around and many of them have surface-to-air rockets." He yanked the yoke to the left, pushed it down hard and sent the Piper into a dizzying spiral-dive.

Flavio was being puerile. "Nah-Nah rockets, you can't catch me!"

Despite the inappropriate comments and roller coaster ride, Otto managed to suppress his rising stomach contents.

At 200 metres Flavio pulled the yoke back to level the aeroplane for the final approach. The makeshift landing strip was desperately short. It was marked with giant trees at both ends and a shockingly rutted surface pock marked with old mortar craters. Could he land without flipping?

"Gott!" Otto yelled above the engine noise,

even though he had not been inside a church for decades. Sweating, he gulped and swallowed his rising stomach contents.

Cowboy Flavio liked a good joke and lived life hard. He set the flaps and backed off the throttle. "Touch down in 50 metres." The undercarriage kissed the treetops, causing the aeroplane to jerk. Otto closed his eyes while Flavio's jaw jutted forward and his eyes were firmly fixed on what seemed an impossible landing. There was no room for error.

"Gott in Himmel!" Otto imagined the worst outcome.

"Just cleaned the undercarriage!" Flavio glanced at Otto as they cleared the last tree. "Hang on!" He killed the power and pulled back on the yoke. The aeroplane flared. The army of trees at the end of the runway marched menacingly towards the little aircraft suspended on a cushion of black air that suddenly deflated, dropping the aeroplane unceremoniously to the ground. As if hit by a jackhammer the aeroplane slowed reacting to the punches from the rutted ground stopping two metres from an immense tree trunk.

The young pilot Ribas turned to Otto. "Welcome to Angola Mr von Eschen. I hope that you enjoyed your flight!" Otto alighted and promptly fell to his knees apparently paying homage to Angolan soil. He vomited.

He was alive but half wished he wasn't. The other men in fatigues walked off into the gloaming.

Flavio giggled. "That was an easy one!" Otto wondered what a difficult flight would be like. He made a note to himself not to fly with Flavio Ribas again.

Otto was in deepest darkest Africa now. It was stifling, close and clammy. The smell of the earth, smoke from the fires around the camp and burned tobacco in the heavy air was oppressive, particularly with the intrusive sounds of frogs, insects and other seething life. The jungle has the highest concentration of wildlife on the planet where nothing is as it appears. Venomous creatures masquerade as leaf litter and insects carry fatal diseases. Here you didn't look at nature – it looked at you.

Darkness approached. All that could be seen of the predatory humans was the whites of their eyes. Groups of soldiers sat around well-established fires. Their drunken mumbled conversation added to the jungle symphony. Cigarettes were passed around among the sociopaths that drank home brew.

Suddenly young Brian Kelly, Babs' second in command, appeared seemingly out of nowhere. Brian was the only white in the camp. He was muscular, lean and taller than average. He smiled with a tic at the corner of his mouth through his alcohol-aged face. The other corner held a half smoked Camel cigarette. Otto wondered how many others were watching from the deep dark damp shadows.

"Major Angula will join us in a while." Brian was a young mercenary with an Australian accent. "I'll show you to the HQ mate." He turned and walked toward the lights. He had a pack of Camels cinched in his olive singlet just above a tattoo of a fist. He lit another cigarette while walking quickly to a large canvas tent with pools of artificial light at its entrance. His short brush cut hair glowed orange.

They ambled past a soldier hanging a goat from a tree. With a rusty machete he split open the belly and eviscerated it. Blood gushed onto the dust; it turned from red to a dark brown jelly. Topless women cooked not far away unaware of the Mzungu in their midst. Nobody cared. The soldiers, now well intoxicated on local brew, randomly fired their AK-47s at empty tins and imaginary enemies.

Brian pointed to an open ammunition box. It was filled with shrivelled pieces of what appeared to be dried meat. It sat on top of crates containing rocket propelled grenades and mortar shells. "We have trophies from our enemies!"

Otto was not interested. "Freeze-dried rations?"

"No, the ears of MPLA soldiers we killed. We call them souven-ears!" Brian closed the box as nonchalantly as you would a toy chest. This got

Otto's attention as he remembered the newscast and vomited again.

Brian ignored Otto's puke. "We use many ways to make the buggers talk! We tow them naked behind a jeep – some last only 50 metres before they talk. Some others we push the barrel of the gun up their a...a... they talk very quickly! The best part," Brian's eyes widened, "comes after they have sung their story. We tell them, 'Okay, you helped us, you can go now, run!' And then they run. And then we shoot them! This is war, meu amigo. Fuck those MPLA bastards. Then we take our souvenirs!"

A few drops of water gave little warning of the torrent about to douse them. The water instantly drowned the dust while puddles formed within seconds. Nothing was dry. Luckily they were now under the heavy canvas of the HQ and sheltered from the deafening downpour. A huge young man covered in an army issue poncho ran in through the waterfall at the tent entrance.

Babs filled the entrance. He was sixteen years old and now a Major.

Dripping and out of breath Babs boomed in a seductive *basso profundo* voice. "Welcome to UNITA!" His pearly teeth flashed a gold inlay. The vibrant inquisitive eyes of his past had faded into the bloodshot abyss of numbness – they were empty. He didn't feel. He didn't care. He was only interested in his wealth and was only motivated by greed.

Babs nodded toward the refectory table and bench. "Dinner! We always look after our guests!"

Otto was pale. He thought of the goat slaughter he saw on arrival and he didn't feel like eating. The soup was thin; just bones with little meat surrounded by a navy of red chilli. He looked at his plate sighed and let his shoulders sag.

"Not hungry?" Babs leaned forward and towered above his small insignificant underweight visitor.

"I get airsick." Otto explained trying to hide his gustatory disgust.

The rain was easing. Tendrils of hot jungle steam rose from the forest. The humidity made the air treacle-like. Otto felt tired, physically and mentally.

"Okay Otto. Let's get down to business. I need to move some diamonds." Otto raised his left eyebrow and his eyes grew bigger. Babs gave no indication as to where these stones were purloined or the human cost in obtaining them.

"With these diamonds I'll buy munitions and we'll both get rich! I have prepared you a special overnight bag for your return to Windhoek. Once you have retrieved the goods from the false bottom you will place them in a deposit box I have at the bank. The key for the box is with the diamonds."

"Ja. Which bank?" Babs winced at the sound of this feeble German speaking English with a tainted Germanic sandpapered falsetto. "Bank Windhoek on Independence Avenue."

Otto nodded. "Okay. What about the safety deposit box number und whose name do I use?"

"I have had a new account opened in your business's name. You need to see Aaron Gough to complete the paperwork. Don't worry. He's trustworthy and has been paid to keep his mouth shut."

"This is where your expertise comes in. You will cut the diamonds and sell them. You will appraise their value in the rough, which you will pay me. The mark up that you make cutting and selling is yours." He moved forward with a large fake grin and his bloodshot eyes said, "I assume that you will give me fair market price." He was not laughing. Otto was not in control anymore.

Otto held out his limp-wristed hand. "Agreed." Babs paw crushed his insignificant member and Otto tried not to wince but failed. Babs was in charge.

Babs opened his arms and welcomed him. "Stay for the night!" He was concerned for Otto's safety, not for Otto's sake but for his blood diamonds. "You can see for yourself we have lots of food, beer, women – everything a man could ever need. Then you go home tomorrow." There was no way that Otto would hear Wagner tonight in this den of iniquity.

Otto unsuccessfully declined. Flavio was the only one who could fly him back to Windhoek. "C'mon Otto, I want to stay. Trust me! You'll have a great time tonight! Besides, it'll be safer to leave in the morning. It's cooled down too much already and I don't think we'll get enough lift for the aeroplane to clear the trees."

Otto deeply suspected safety had little to do with Flavio's reluctance to leave; more like an appetite for goat, booze and sex. Brian gave a twitching grin of someone going insane. He probably was.

Babs leaned back and laughed culminating in a clap of human thunder. All activity in the camp stopped. Babs had spoken.

Babs opened his mouth to speak. "Brian–"

Then all hell broke lose.

Mortar rounds peppered the ground shedding deadly red streaks of shrapnel with the rapidity of Chinese crackers. The explosions concussed the ears of all. Otto flinched with each pounding explosion. He used his Swiss army knife to cut through his money belt. As it fell to the ground, he gutted it like an eel revealing $2,500 US dollars. After the shortest haggle on record, the scared looking Flavio settled for a $1,750 bribe to leave right away.

They ran to the aeroplane. The small aircraft danced to the resounding force of the mortar shells as the two pushed the Piper back into the trees for a few extra metres of runway. Zing! Something red rocketed past Otto's face. Flavio ducked. Otto felt a hot rush in his left knee. The pain radiated out of the site where shrapnel had entered. His eyes widened and brow furrowed.

"Scheisse! – Gott im Himmel – I'm hit!"

Oddly enough the wound did not bleed. Flavio threw Otto's diamond filled bag into the cabin behind the pilot's seat and heaved the wounded Otto into the co-pilot's seat. Otto's contorted face was pale and speechless. Flavio ran around to the left side of the aeroplane and jumped in. The engine spluttered to life. It shuddered and screamed at full throttle. Flavio released the brake to slingshot the aeroplane out of this black hole back to Namibia.

Only metres from apparent obliteration, Otto saw the airspeed reach 70 knots. His mouth dropped open and his eyes bulged. Flavio ripped back the yoke. The trees let the spinning wheels pass. The engine settled into regular drone. Once out of the range of rocket fire, Flavio levelled out and eased off the throttle.

Otto's aircraft nausea had left him to be replaced by searing pain. He used his handkerchief to apply pressure to the wound but it hurt too much. Without warning Otto retched again as acidic chili burned his throat. The red bloodstain saturated his pants.

In less than a couple of hours Otto was back in Windhoek.

Elspeth was there to greet the aeroplane as it parked in the hanger. Flavio disembarked and whispered something in her ear and left the hangar. She opened the right door and her jaw dropped at the sight of his leg.

"What happened to your leg Mr von Eschen?"

Otto pressed his fist to his lips and grimaced. "Pieces of metal."

"Let's get you out." She looked for help but Flavio had left the hangar.

"Hold my hand." Otto held out his left two-digit hand. He lifted his legs out of the cockpit with the assistance of his good hand. He tried to slide to the ground below but it was too far. He jumped and landed on his right leg and wobbled. Elspeth supported him as he used his other hand to hold onto the aircraft. A lightning bolt of pain sped from his leg through his spine to his brain. He took a step back and his eyebrows snapped open – he was gobsmacked with the pain that seared his brain.

Elspeth empathised with his pain. "Let's get you seated."

Flavio returned with a wheelchair.

"HALT!" Otto screamed. "I've left my bag in the aeroplane!" His pallid contorted face glistened as a backdrop for his panicking eyes.

Flavio walked nonchalantly towards Otto swinging the bag. Otto held his left leg. It would not bend but oozed blood gluing his trousers to the wound.

"I thought you might like this!" Flavio threw the small bag to Otto. Otto caught the bag. He grimaced with on impact but put on a forced smile. His leg throbbed and the bloodstain enlarged.

"Danke schoen!" Otto clenched his teeth. He imagined what would happen had the overnight bag gone missing. He held the inanimate object like a precious child and let out a sigh of relief.

Elspeth helped him from the wheelchair to the little VW. He got in with great difficulty and pain. Each move drove the shrapnel deeper into the joint. It hurt too much for him to swear so Elspeth suggested going to the hospital. Otto declined.

After arriving at the house, Otto gently eased himself out of the car and slowly reached a standing position. He sucked in air through his teeth, and then dismissed Elspeth and she left. He stood there, wobbled and looked toward the front door. The embedded shrapnel grated against the inner workings of his knee so every time he moved the joint he cried out. Would he make it?

Unable to move forward, Otto turned around and 'walked' backward, dragging his injured leg until he finally entered the house.

He opened the overnight bag. The false bottom was difficult to recognise but the Swiss army knife did its job. He pushed the office swivel chair on casters to the office door entrance. He pulled back the carpet and yelped and opened the safe embedded in the concrete slab.

He wiped his hand down his sweaty face as he realised that it was a mistake to refuse Elspeth's offer. The lightning bolts of pain showered his body. Nauseous and giddy, he fainted landing next to his office chair.

He woke looking at the bookshelves sideways and saw the open safe. He squirmed towards the bag with the diamonds and cried out; the bag but it was out of reach. Less than a metre away it seemed as far away as the moon. He lay there whimpering and took a deep breath then slowly swam to the bag using his elbows, dragging his legs behind. Five minutes later – "Got it!" He exclaimed, then rolled onto his back and tried to breathe the pain away. He placed the diamonds in the safe, closed the door and turned the tumbler. He could not feel his legs anymore.

Otto needed help.

He rolled over and looked at the ceiling searching for the answer to his predicament. Unfortunately he had left his mobile in the cradle.

Looking at the chair, engineer Otto recognised the problem at hand. The chair had wheels that made it easy to move but difficult to use as a support. He pulled himself up using the desk, slid over to the bookshelves and standing on one leg grabbed the back of the chair.

He stopped and the pain hit him – "Scheisse!!!!" then moved slowly to the entrance using the chair as a walker.

The Land Cruiser was so close yet so far. Each Everest step got him a little closer. Unfortunately, the chair was not cooperating so he sat and looked at his knee where the bloodstain was larger and ran into his socks. He slipped onto the garage floor letting out a high-pitched scream before losing consciousness. He awoke woozy and disoriented.

Otto cursed then looked at himself for damage. None. He tried again. He hung onto the mirror and clenched his teeth. Carefully he lifted himself backwards into the vehicle sliding his buttocks onto the smooth leather seats and, lifting his knees he swung his legs inside. The pain was too much. He lost consciousness for a heartbeat. He fumbled; eventually he keyed the starter and the truck sprung to life, the V8 gurgling like a kid chugging a soft drink. He drove to the Windhoek Central Hospital.

They gave him orders for antibiotics, a walking stick and instructions for rest, but he did not obey any of them. Next day he deposited the diamonds in the Bank Windhoek and a month later the diamonds were cut. He had found buyers for the 247 carats of glittering stones; Babs and Otto became insanely rich.

And this was just the beginning.

The Proposal

Otto snapped out of his colourful but painful memory and snatched the silver dollar mid flight. He put it back in his pocket, looked down at his knee and sighed. It was because of Babs he would never walk normally again. He had considered knee surgery but Otto had tomophobia, a fear of surgery. One day he would get it done. Babs was pain but his money was relief, or so he thought. Babs had given Otto his private number. He dialled the number, which seemed to take an inordinate time to answer.

It was 13:01.

He made a fruitless effort to use the deepest voice he could muster. "Hello Babs. Otto von Eschen. How are you?"

Nobody could forget Babs' voice. "Very well thank you."

"It has been a while hasn't it?"

"Let's get down to business." Babs talked and Otto listened intently with his head cocked. The clock raced past 13:20. His eyes danced: scintillating reflections of the Vikings past. He looked at his leg. Did he want more pain from this man? At least he could find out what he wanted.

"Augenblick! I'll look in my agenda. Yes. Lunch at Joe's April 30th at midday, I'll be there."

"Bring your plans!"

"Auf Wiedersehen Babs."

Otto terminated the call and looked at Sparkle. He lit another cigarette. Taking a deep breath Otto looked at his knee. "Time for some anaesthetic," he said as he limped to the kitchen and got his Schnapps bottle. He sat in the chair and drank straight from the bottle. It was not physical pain that controlled his life; it was emotional pain with its elusive answer. Babs was not the answer.

He had not learned his lesson.

Babs Sets the Agenda

Otto parked his Land Cruiser in Joe's parking lot, locked it and paid the guard. He looked at his mobile. It was 11:30 in the morning. With his Boer hat covering his self-proclaimed 'sandy' hair he placed his prescription sunglasses over his crooked nose and slowly limped toward the gates of Joe's Beerhouse. He mopped his sweaty wrinkled brow with a damp handkerchief. As he needed a table with shade and away from others, he had booked a semi-secluded table shaded by a thatched roof in the front opposite the gift shop. Total privacy could not be assured.

He sat down and using his damaged hand placed his paisley cane on the ground. He had been informed that this practise would bring bad luck, but he did not believe in luck or God, just Otto von Eschen. He wiped his allergic eyes - Acacia pollen. He might have appeared a wimp but such an assumption would be a serious error.

The wind revealed his comb over, the grey locks hung to the side. He saw his reflection on the sliding doors and went into a dream. The flash of his diamond ear stud, a souvenir of the first time he met Babs, snapped him out of it. He examined his image in the glass and did not like what he saw.

He pulled out his shiny silver dollar. This coin was precious to him. He had received it as a 'gift' from a German who saw fit to pay Otto in silver. He started flipping it remembering what Babs was like so many years ago. He thought of his bloated bank accounts and the number of offshore properties that he owned because of Babs. However, he could not, and would not, forget the severed ears.

He stopped dreaming and looked at his mobile again. Babs was now late, a habit that he kept for most of his meetings. Otto took off his glasses and cleaned them with an unused handkerchief. He scrunched up his face accentuating the degree of his hooked broken nose. Otto was always fastidiously punctual.

He ordered a beer, a cold beautifully quaffable amber Windhoek Lager. The sweat on his brow matched the condensation on the glass. He gulped the beer and emptied his first pint before the waiter had returned to his station, and then he sighed, lit a cigarette and let his shoulders relax for just a moment before checking the time again. It was 12:21. He continued to fumble through the menu nervously, even though he could recite its contents blind.

Babs lumbered through the gates to the appointed spot where Otto was draining the last of his second pint. He arose to greet him giving his typical Captain Hook like gesture to the chair opposite.

Babs may not have had the superior intelligence of Otto, but his adequate intelligence was matched with a behemoth body, strength and power. Since last they met he had filled out and had a round face, menacing bloodshot eyes and the scar on his left cheek had contracted changing his pseudo smile to one that was unnerving, more serious – lethal.

"Guten tag." Otto said in a muffled alto voice as he ran his fingers through his hair. "How are things in Luanda?"

"Very good." Babs' voice vibrated the table. He laughed, stopping all conversation at Joe's. Few have mistaken this convivial laughter as charm. Underneath lies a scorpion ready to use its tail: a deadly Santa Claus.

Otto rubbed his old war wound and straightened his back. "Is that old wound still giving you trouble?" Babs perfectly disguised his lack of empathy for Otto's plight let alone his disdain for such a decrepit human being.

Otto crossed his arms. "I am not a schlappschwanz! I hurt but I am no wuss! I am considering surgery."

Babs was like a foghorn. "Get off your high horse Otto. I was only trying to be polite. I want to hear your plan for stealing the 727-300 that we discussed."

Babs' mobile phone cut the conversation. He listened then terminated the call.

"We now have a target that will fit our plans. My colleague in Luanda confirmed the following: there is a 727-300 cargo-plane. It has been sitting on the runway idle for the last 14 months accruing more than $4 million in backdated airport fees and apparently the aircraft is in beautiful condition. It's recently been fitted with new engines."

Babs leaned back giving a half moon smile. "Let's go through the plan you have for stealing it and I shall ensure that you have all the resources you need to make it happen. What do you think it is worth on the black market?"

Otto rubbed his hands together. "The engines are almost new with less than 1,000 compression cycles on them. They're not even run in! Such new engines should bring half of a million dollars each, so we'll make more than one million dollars after expenses!" He straightened his back, put his chin up, and handed Babs a large four-ringed binder bulging with print divided by multiple tabs of various colours.

"I have a number of scenarios mapped out. I believe scenario C 'Charlie' is the best. You have a copy of the strategy, plan, materials, execution, management und costs in your binder.

"You will be working with Flavio Ribas and Brian Kelly. Do you remember flying with Flavio? He was your pilot when you came to visit me back in '76. I know he can be a jerk at times, but I trust him and his flying is second to none.

You might also remember Brian from your trip to visit me? He showed you around and made you feel comfortable at the camp. Did I ever tell you that he's a mercenary from Australia?"

"Yes, I do remember the two. My knee will never forget!" Otto looked at the strands of light shining through the leaves onto the table. "How can I forget the ears?"

"I think we have time on our side with this one." Babs held his jaw. "The aeroplane has been sitting on the tarmac for ages and the legal issues surrounding the aircraft have not been sorted out. It's not guarded very well." Otto looked through Babs and imagined the aeroplane. He flipped his coin harder than ever.

Otto pursed his lips. "So you still have the original destination in mind?"

Babs leaned toward Otto and placed his massive paw around his shoulder. He gave the employee a beguiling grin. "This aeroplane will be taking a one-way trip. I have a team setup in the hinterlands of Democratic Republic of Congo (DRC) who are making a temporary runway in the bush. I think the only thing of value in the aeroplane is the engines, do you agree?"

"Yes. The return on investment for other parts is poor, if any." Otto bit his finger.

Otto gestured toward the open folder on Babs' knees. "In the documentation you will find the personnel requirements und equipment that we shall need to get the aeroplane to the DRC. I have even included timeline und milestones for the disassembly. I assume that you will be handling the DRC end?" Otto looked up over the top of his glasses.

"Yes. Anything else at this time?" Babs was winding up the meeting.

"Nein."

Babs beckoned to the driver who came and opened the doors. The men unfolded and headed back into Joe's. Babs sat down first as Otto scratched around like an old hen trying to find a comfortable position for his leg. Once settled, he lit a cigarette.

Otto tilted his head to the side. "When would you like to do the heist?" He was almost inaudible.

Babs looked to the sky, looked down at his belly and then looked into those watery gimlet eyes. "Let's try for the third week of May. The runway in the DRC will be finished by then and I don't want the site discovered. We should aim for May 26th or around that date."

Otto thumped the table. "But that's only three weeks away!"

Babs did not react. "Otto. You are so organised and have this operation planned in beautiful detail. I would expect that you could start right away!"

Otto blinked a couple of times, pulled out his silver dollar and started flipping it again. "Of course I can start right away Babs. I was just a little surprised that we have a green light for operation Charlie so soon." Otto sat back in his chair and ran his fingers through his hair and blew smoke rings upward.

They both contemplated their beer. Otto looked up. "Well Babs, I should meet with Flavio und Brian as soon as possible."

"That is why I brought them down with me! I've put them up in the Kalahari Sands."

Otto lifted his arms. "Wunderbar!" He then raised his glass and spoke deliberately so as not to slur his words. "Here's to health und happiness - Prost!"

Babs smiled and whispered in Otto's ear. "And lots of money. Don't forget the money!"

They finished their drinks and left for the Kalahari Sands hotel – in separate cars of course.

Operation Charlie

Otto drunkenly parked opposite the Kalahari Sands and swung his legs out of the car. He stood unsteadily hanging onto the mirror and realised that he shouldn't have driven. With briefcase in tow, he crossed Independence Avenue at the robot displaying a green walk sign, entered the Kalahari Sands complex, and hobbled to the lift just past the tourist trap stores.

His awkward gait did not draw attention as he often visited the Kalahari Sands for business meetings. He got off the elevator at the first floor and hobbled over to the reception desk for the hotel. He ordered a young Asian looking woman from the Nama tribe. "Get me Flavio Ribas und Brian Kelly."

The cute girl recoiled and tried not to grimace. She smiled with a gold glint from one of her healthy front teeth: fashion. "Just one moment sir."

"I have Brian Kelly on the line for you sir." Otto informed Brian that he was coming up to their room. The Boss had arrived. He stumbled drunkenly, gave the receiver back to the receptionist and then looked down his nose at her. "Vielen Dank."

The elevator doors opened on the 2nd floor. Otto used the wall for support. He steadied himself and knocked on the door. Brian, stinking of cigarette smoke opened the door with the safety chain attached. He released the chain and greeted Otto.

Brian tried to break the ice. "So Babs says we're on an operation together?"

Otto remembered his closeness to Babs in the Angolan jungle. "Babs said that he would arrive later und he wants to make sure you are up to the job und we have all we need for the operation." Otto stood while Brian sat in submission.

"Where is Flavio?"

"You know Flavio! He's in the casino probably with a beautiful girl hanging off his shoulder. I'll go get him if you like."

"Ja. Danke." Otto was relieved to sit down. He turned off the TV, tossed the remote onto the bed and removed the laptop from his briefcase.

Gantt charts and other planning materials appeared on the screen. The thought of operation Charlie sent a wave of excitement throughout his alcohol soaked body. He fanned himself with the room service menu and mumbled. The mechanical whir of the door lock stopped his soliloquy and heralded the arrival of the other two conspirators.

"Guten Tag Flavio. Did you have any success at the casino?" His blue impaling eyes were accentuated by an artificial smile.

"Yes. I won 500 Namibian dollars!" Flavio ran his fingers over the edge of the cash. "I'm on a lucky roll! Here's to a successful job!" Brian looked closely at the cash and then at Flavio and then smiled.

Otto jerked back into action. "We have a lot of work to do." Otto had removed his coin and was flipping it enthusiastically. He felt like a schoolboy winning the class prize for initiative: the perfect plan. "On May 26th we shall be stealing a 727-300 fuel freighter from Luanda. Flavio and Brian will fly the aeroplane into the Democratic Republic of the Congo. There the aeroplane will be stripped for parts. Operation Charlie looks like this." Otto turned the screen to the others showing the silver 'T'-tailed vehicle.

He reached into his briefcase to retrieve two four-ringed binders identical to the one he gave to Babs at lunch. "In your folder you will find a detailed copy of operation Charlie. I'll give you one hour to familiarise yourself with the material." Flavio and Brian looked at each other, frowned then shrugged their shoulders.

Brian tried to hide the fact that the last thing he read was Playboy two years ago. "Crikey mate! That's a bloody lot of material to read in an hour!"

"I'm sure you'll do just fine." Otto gave one of his most denigrating looks through his intoxicated eyes. "I presume that Babs has told you about your pay?"

"Yes!" Their greedy eyes glittered with the thought of what they could buy.

Otto got up drunkenly. "I shall see you gentleman in an hour." He limped out the door using the furniture for support.

Flavio suspected that Brian was illiterate. "Otto has divided the tasks into airport security, refuelling, embarking, securing the aeroplane, disabling the transponder, flight plan, and radio communication."

"Tell me about the security." Brian knew that was part of his job. "Do I have to silence anyone?"

"No. Babs has taken care of security giving us a window of 30 minutes to get the aeroplane out of there." Flavio was well aware of Brians' ability to be violent. "Babs says that its owners will refuel the aeroplane. They're going to test the engines. I don't know how Babs got his information, but the 727 will have 53,000 litres of jet fuel giving us a range of about 2,400 kilometres." Flavio nodded slowly and pulled his right ear.

"Okay. Next point?" Brian keenly looked at the incomprehensible sheet.

Flavio pointed to a passage from his briefing package. "The owner of the aircraft has a pilot set to test the engines on the morning of May 27th. We'll take the aeroplane late afternoon on the 26th. We'll walk across the tarmac nonchalantly like any other employee so as not to draw attention.

Entry should be easy because the rear gangway will be down. Next you will secure the aeroplane using whatever means necessary."

"My task is to fly the aeroplane. I shall need you to sit in the co-pilot's seat for take off and landing." He opened a picture of the cockpit. Brian's jaw dropped and his heart missed a beat. He was out of his depth and couldn't swim; so many instruments.

Brian raised an eyebrow and gave a smirk. "When are you going to give me flying lessons?"

"Your job is to assist me with the controls and that is ALL – get it?" Flavio got up to get another beer.

"The next item is our flight plan." Flavio looked at the picture of the African savannah hanging on the wall above the bed. He was actually visualizing the jungle and his mind was flying the proposed route. He snapped out of his daydream and looked at Brian's puppy like expression.

"I have been instructed to fly the aeroplane directly northwest for 30 minutes then change course northeast to the DRC. There will be no radio communications with air traffic control. They can't track us as I shall turn off the transponder." Brian sat there looking as blank as the television screen he was staring at. "You and I are going to land the jet in the DRC forest. Otto will give me the exact coordinates tomorrow."

The lock whirred and Babs filled the doorway. "Good afternoon gentlemen!" The thunder rolled in squashing them into submission.

"Where's Otto?" Babs scowled.

"I think he went downstairs for coffee sir."

"Brian. Go get Otto on the double!" Babs did not seem to be in a good mood.

The lock whirred again and Otto limped in followed by Brian. Brian's tic matched his deranged look. Otto lit a cigarette then passed the lighter to Brian. Babs did not smoke. Brian thought better than to light up a Camel as Babs detested the smell of cigarettes, particularly Otto's brand. He looked directly into Otto's subdued eyes and lifted his eyebrows. The cigarette hardly had a chance to ignite before its hopes were crushed in the ashtray.

Babs sat down by the desk. "I want you to give me the details of the job in your own words Flavio."

Flavio gave a step-by-step account of the heist and confirmed with Babs that there would be a ground power unit available for engine start. Babs also assured him that there would be no one on the aeroplane. Flavio then enquired about the runway.

"It's about two thousand metres. There will be 'runway lights' to guide you." Babs marked the parentheses in the air. "It will be packed but rough." Flavio scratched his head and closed his eyes imagining a treetop disaster.

Babs concluded the meeting. "As I already told you, I shall pay you in US dollars when the aeroplane has been safely delivered to the DRC and the engines have been sold. As you will be flying back to Luanda from Kinshasa, I'll meet you at my house for a meal. You will leave with your brick of cash in a brown paper bag. It will be a celebration of our success, so come hungry!"

He turned his focus to Otto. "Otto, if you don't need anything more from me I shall wish you gentleman good luck and I hope to hear that you have successfully landed in the DRC and that salvage operations have begun."

Otto avoided Babs' stare. "Yes sir! Alles in Ordnung." Babs ducked while passing through the doorway, a habit that he developed over the years. He buttoned his jacket hiding most of the starched white shirt highlighted with a paisley tie.

Flavio was worried. "What about landing? I don't like the idea of a rough airstrip. I could lose the undercarriage and that would not do the side engines any good. I can't guarantee that the old bird will stay on her pins if the strip is too rough. It's not Babs' Piper!"

"That's why Babs chose you for the job. He believes in you and your abilities to land the prize safely."

Otto wrapped up the meeting. "I expect you both to have memorised the plan by May 19th, Verstehen?"

They did a quick nod as they got up keen to leave the closed, smoky, claustrophobic room.

The 727's days were numbered.

B727-300 is Stolen

The trip to Luanda the day before had been straightforward. They had exited the dilapidated airport that smelled of mould, sweat, spilled beer and stale cigarette smoke in the azure Angolan air hanging heavily with humidity. They stayed the night at the Hotel Presidente.

It was morning and Al Jazeera was bursting with energy not expected for the hour. Otto terminated the broadcast. "Have you heard from the airstrip?" Flavio smiled and sighed when Otto nodded.

"Everything is in place. Now just follow your checklists. Flavio?"

"Yes sir?"

"The aeroplane's code name is 'Seabird' und the base 'Charlie.' They will be listening for you at the specified UHF setting." Flavio pointed to the line on his checklist.

The humidity hit the trio like a wet steaming towel as they left the hotel; perspiration was almost instantaneous. Horns honked in the disorder of Luanda. Brian carried the small carry-on containing blue overalls with embroidered TAAG on the shoulder and left breast pocket. Flavio hailed a taxi. The taxi screeched to a halt. "Airport!"

"Obrigado!" Otto handed the taxi driver double the normal cab fair. The driver in his mid twenties did a double take and quickly pocketed the kwanza.

After arriving at the airport, they ate a disgusting expensive hamburger at midday in the cafeteria. "This is gross!" Flavio threatened to spit out the offending morsel.

"You're not the one paying $45 for them. Don't complain. We'll meet back here at 16:45."

It was 16:48 when Otto entered the code for the secure staff entrance to the inner airport. The door closed after them with a loud clonk; an ominous sound – the point of no return. The dilapidated appearance inside the terminal was no match for the degeneration in the bowels of the airport; chaos would be an understatement.

They saw the sentry at the baggage entrance at the side of a large rollup door. His weapon was facing down with the safety on. Hiding behind a pile of detritus the team changed into their overalls. Otto remained dressed as a businessman. It was now 16:52. All they had to do was wait.

As planned, as close to 17:00 as African time would allow, the guard left his post leaving a clear path to the tarmac. They could see the T-tail marked with the letters N844AA and the old American Airlines colour scheme.

Flavio and Brian walked calmly to the aeroplane and mounted the tail entrance ladder and were hit with a strong smell of diesel fuel.

The inside was totally gutted except for the fuel tanks. There was no way that this vehicle could be returned to a state fit for passengers. Flavio started his pilot's checklist while Brian kept guard.

"Uh-oh."

"What Brian?"

"Two bogies coming from the building - show time!" It was now 17:15. The real crew was not supposed to be there until the next morning. Brian prepared for violence when the pilots boarded. They didn't stand a chance. With a single twist, Brian broke their necks leaving their bodies convulsing. "What's going on back there," asked Flavio?

Brian laughed. "Oh, just the old chooks are flapping."

"Gross!" Flavio paused momentarily. "Don't touch their ears!"

"Yup." Brian moved the bodies out of the aisle and then entered the cockpit. "Flavio what do you want me to do?"

"Sit in the chair and buckle up. Here is the checklist. Read the list down from 'flaps ¾.'"

"P-ar-king brrr-ake ON"

Flavio grabbed his list. "Give that to me or we shall be here 'til tomorrow!" He read the list and stopped. "I thought you could read a little bit. Put your headset on." Flavio finished the list skipping two items: identification lights ON and transponder ON.

The hamster cage started to rotate slowly then increased in speed. "Fuel ignition switch ON." Flavio flipped a switch initiating a roar of ignited fuel. The engine rapidly increased in pitch and volume. The blue smoke of unburned fuel lasted only a couple of seconds. Flavio started the other two engines and pushed the three throttles forward. The pitch of the engines increased and the jet moved forward. The hum of the electronics and cockpit machinery mixed with the pungent odour of distillate brought Brian back to times in a helicopter on the way to a mission.

The radio crackled and Air Traffic Control came through loud and clear. *"N844AA you are not cleared for take off. N844AA–"* Flavio interjected.

"ATC we are just testing the engines." He changed the frequency before ground control could reply.

"Okay Brian. Let's go test these engines!"

Flavio's face had a grin of a child starting a roller coaster ride as he pushed the three throttle levers forward to their maximum. The engines spooled up pushing them back in their seats as the thrust increased. He liked this aeroplane.

Flavio pulled back on the yoke detaching the jet from the ground. "Boy this thing is powerful!" The ground fell away. "But what a gas guzzler." The black contrails confirmed his comment.

Flavio moved the undercarriage lever to the up position. Seabird's appendages clunked home and the doors clamped shut and the noise level dropped. "Once we level out you'll see nothing but sea." Flavio reassured Brian as he retracted the flaps. He backed off the throttles and levelled out a little. They reached a cruising altitude of 30,000 feet.

Flavio looked at his watch. "I estimate arrival and touch down in the DRC at about 19:55. I just hope the runway is not too soft." Flavio adjusted the radio frequency.

"This is Seabird calling Charlie. Come in Charlie. Over"

A heavily accented voice replied. "Seabird this is Charlie. Over."

"Charlie I read you 5 by 5. Request permission to land at base, over."

"Permission granted. What's your ETA, over?"

Flavio looked at his watch. "ETA is in 75 minutes. I repeat ETA in one hour 15 minutes. Over."

"Message received. Land from the east. Wind 10 knots west. Over."

"Charlie this is Seabird. WILCO. Over and out."

As the sun said goodnight, the dark blue ocean metamorphosed into dark mounds of jungle. The undulating green decayed to sinister black as the sun reflected off the remaining treetops still illuminated: pebbles on a black beach.

An hour passed quietly until Flavio broke the silence taking the aeroplane off autopilot and pulling back on the throttles.

"Brian. Get ready for descent and landing."

"Okay. But what do I do?"

Flavio pointed to the airspeed and altitude gauges. "I want you to read the numbers on those two dials. You can read numbers can't you?"

"Of course I can."

"Okay. Give them to me."

Brian's ears popped. "Airspeed 450 and altitude 11,000… Airspeed 440 and altitude 9500." Brian pulled his ears.

"Straight ahead!" Brian was pointing to the illuminated tracks in front that had suddenly appeared. "Christ, the ground is coming up fast!"

Landing lights lit up the mist in front of the aeroplane. "Numbers!"

"Airspeed 298 altitude 1950."

"Charlie this is Seabird. Come in Charlie. Over."

"Seabird this is Charlie. Over."

"Charlie this is Seabird. On final approach ETA two minutes. Over."

With nose up, flaps fully extended and undercarriage down they floated then dropped onto the makeshift runway. Flavio wrestled with the yoke as the runway pulled on the undercarriage. The front undercarriage could not resist the trauma and collapsed.

The aeroplane stopped. The front wheel was partially bent backward, but the engines were untouched. "We made it Brian! No damage." Flavio shut off the fuel and then gave Brian a high five. The jungle swarmed with people like vultures surrounding fresh carrion. Machinery appeared from the dark as the engines spun down. A generator chuffed then settled down to a regular throb. Suddenly the area was flood lit.

Brian lowered the rear stairway. A man dressed in army fatigues greeted them and pointed to a white truck sitting at the edge of the cleared jungle. "Your lift is over there." The floodlit site was now seething with activity and the din of heavy equipment. Already the lift was under one of the engines and the Catherine wheel from cutting equipment lit up the surrounding trees.

Flavio broke the silence. He pushed his luxuriant growth of dark curly hair out of his eyes and turned to the soldier. "What will they do with the scrap?"

"The aeroplane will be covered with a camouflage net and the jungle will consume it before it is found, if it's ever found." He focused on the activities at the aeroplane. "Move out of the way so we can get on with our job. Your driver is waiting."

They arrived at 05:30 at the airport in plenty of time to catch their 09:50 flight to Luanda. The flight from Kinshasa to Luanda was uneventful and surprisingly quick in comparison to the travel of the night before.

Operation Charlie was a success.

Celebration

The gang arrived at Babs' home and the sound of an assault rifle being cocked was unmistakable. "AK-47." Brian had heard the sound many times before.

The guard let the vehicle through, waving his rifle like a toreador's foil. They crossed what appeared to be a small-scale railway track. The grounds were beautiful, about five hectares in all. The house had winding cobblestone paths to the car park and to the pool. Next to it was a gazebo with a dinner table replete with fruit and exotic nuts. Two candelabras were unnecessarily lit in the blazing Angolan sun.

Babs rose from his chair, opened his arms to greet them and then slapped Otto on the back. Brian wondered whether Otto's bent form could take such a blow. "Come and sit down." The trio sat under the gazebo, as two waiters dressed in white seemed to appear from nowhere and offered them refreshments.

Otto and Flavio took champagne and Brian a beer. The waiters quickly brought the drinks to the table. One waiter poured the Dom Perignon champagne for the two while the other an N´gola Cerveja Superior for Brian.

"Okay Otto. Tell me what happened."

"We were successful und all went according to plan. I'll let Flavio und Brian fill you in on the details.

Babs crossed his legs. "Congratulations!"

Flavio went first and described his role in the execution of the heist. "I must admit it was like riding a bucking bronco. But she was a lady and I had her in my arms…" Flavio drifted off into the land of naked women. Otto rolled his eyes.

"Well done Flavio. Now Brian, how many people did you kill? I hope that you didn't take souvenirs!"

Brian described the heist from his point of view impressing Babs that his murders were done efficiently.

Satiated with yet more exquisite fare, they watched intently as Babs pulled out two brick-like paper bags. He gave one to Brian and the other to Flavio. "Well done boys I hope that we can do business again!" Otto relaxed knowing that his reward made theirs look like chump change.

The Opportunity

Chapter 1 - Babs' Dream

Jose had just finished setting up a breakfast buffet beautifully arranged on a table against the back wall under the original Rembrandt that Babs cherished. Babs always insisted on having excess of his needs. A small French polished dining table covered with a damask tablecloth and matching serviettes had been set with solid silver cutlery and the best Royal Dalton china.

Babs sipped his coffee while reading the Aviation Week and Space Technology magazine.

He stopped chewing his morsel and his bloodshot eyes narrowed. He pulled out his reading glasses and couldn't believe his eyes. The title: 'SCARCE 777 PARTS WILL AFFECT AFTERMARKET' jumped out and secured his attention.

He had acquired an interest in TAAG Angola Airlines even though it is 100% owned by the government of Angola. He had the ear of the chairman and CEO and was a sole source contractor. Basically, the CEO gave him a blank cheque to make his problems disappear.

The company was in desperate need of an engine for one of their Boeing 777 fleet of three. This AOG plane (Aircraft on Ground) was threatening corporate survival. He remembered 2003. "I must have Otto von Eschen over to

69

discuss a possible new venture." He had not yet planned a heist, but knew that he would be well compensated for returning the 777 to service. All he needed was an engine. A new one would cost more than the company could handle. He stared out of his glass castle looking past Luanda out beyond the sea up into the sky.

Aviation Week's description of the situation cited 1,073 Boeing 777s in service; five had been scrapped or written off due to accidents and three were in storage. The youth of the fleet and high aircraft values were going to keep parts rare and expensive for quite some time. Babs' grin widened. He looked closer at the article then leaned back in his chair. He looked out the window again and pondered tapping his finger on his bottom lip. "Maybe I need a whole aeroplane for its parts?"

The relationship of supply to demand is a key economic principle – here the demand for parts exceeded supply; hence, the profit from attaining a replacement turbofan would be handsome. The magazine stated that engine parts were the most sought after.

He made a few calls and responded to emails that he thought worthy of his attention and then picked up the magazine and made for the door. "Jose. I'm heading out and will not be back for the rest of the day."

"Yes sir." Jose looked at Babs with amorous eyes. Babs gave him a wink and put up his hand as if to say: enough. "If Otto von Eschen rings send me an SMS."

Otto did call.

Jose did send an SMS.

Otto would be in his office in the morning.

Bar Fight in Coonabarabran

18:20: August 16th 2013 – Coonabarabran Australia

Known as the astronomy capital of Australia and a central area of wheat and sheep farming, Coonabarabran is nestled in the foothills of the Warrumbungles, one of New South Wales' national parks. It's a small town with a population of approximately three thousand and has a number of pubs including the Royal Hotel. Friday night is a time where many Australian workingmen gather at the local pub to discuss sports, Sheilas (girls) and cars. Friday after work was sacrosanct: the boys' 'night out'. Their wives sat at home hoping that there would be something left of the week's pay cheque.

Bruce Kelly dropped out of school at grade eight and was not good with girls. He spent his working life doing general labouring jobs only when he needed money: a twenty first century swagman. He had been working as casual labour in the winter of 2013 employed in the vicinity of Coonabarabran sorting grain. Actually he was working nearer Gilgandra where he usually spent most Friday evenings drinking at the Railway Hotel. The work was hard, dusty and hot but paid well in cash. No questions were asked. He was known as Bruce. This Friday night Bruce decided to visit Coonabarabran as per the advice of one of his mates.

Bruce felt much better after his shower as did his hair that now returned to its native orange colour. The grey was beginning to show his 48 years. He checked his weight and noted that he had dropped a kilo this week and now weighed 97 kilograms for his well-toned 190-centimetre large frame. He dressed quickly wearing shorts, shirt, long socks and Blundstone boots. His broken nose and multiple scars bespoke of a history of violence.

He was tired and the 80 kilometres drive to Coonabarabran seemed to take an eternity. He was thirsty and was going for a beer – not just 'a' beer, rather a number that had yet to be determined.

The car squeaked to a halt in front of the Royal Hotel on John Street and its achy joints groaned as Bruce got out. He looked at the old brick structure with a yellow façade that could use a good coat of paint. Bruce pushed the heavy unoiled front door under the bar sign and entered the smoky room.

'A pub with no beer', immortalised by Slim Dusty, was playing in the background. The TV gave news of the horse races in Sydney and the dartboard was attracting patrons like flies. There was standing room only and he was an outsider. He had not been to the Royal before. There was no welcoming committee. Regulars looked on with suspicion at the stranger who was ordering a beer. "Schooner of Toohey's mate."

The bartender closed the tap and handed him the ice-cold lager foamed to the brim. "That'll be $6.90." The race on TV finished and the rambunctious patrons cheered. Even the dart game paused to see the outcome. Much grumbling and mumbling accompanied the transfer of money from loser to winner.

"Hey, you're new around here aren't you mate?" A middle-aged bald patron moved toward the bar. His missing front teeth indicated he was no stranger to a fight. He squeezed his body nearer the bar and pushed Bruce out of the way. The bar nicely supported his belly but he was wobbly. He turned to look at Bruce with impaired eyes. "What's your name sport?"

"They call me Bruce and I'm just up here for a couple of months."

"They call me Bazza, Barry Luck to be correct. Hey guys! Old carrot top here's name is Bruce."

His mates looked back blankly.

"My name is Bruce – NOT – carrot top!" Bruce was deadly serious now. He thought he should warn those who insulted him. "Just a tip – don't call me carrot top again!" Bruce's face was beetroot and his hair seemed to glow in defiance to Bazza's comment.

"All right carrot top!" This was a bad move on behalf of Bazza. He should never have said that. He was too drunk to realise the impact of what he said.

Bazza didn't see the lethal blow coming. He didn't raise a hand in defence before Bruce's massive fist hit him firmly in the jaw rotating his brain into oblivion. He fell and lay motionless on the tiled floor not breathing. A patron put down his dart. "Someone call the cops!"

Bruce did not wait for the cops to arrive. He pushed by the men gathering to see what had happened, exited and fired up the Holden. He took off in a cloud of blue smoke with squealing tyres, juddering clutch and engine valves bouncing, heading west toward Broken Hill.

Bruce Kelly was now a wanted man.

He drove through the night and had to stop for petrol at dawn. The sun rose and it looked like another day without rain. He bought a newspaper and was horrified to see on the third page 'Fatal Bar Fight over Carrot Top.'

Yesterday at the Royal Hotel in Coonabarabran a pub fight ended with a fatal blow. Barry Luck had been teasing a patron new to the area about his orange hair.

"All he did was to call him 'carrot top'," said one of the patrons. "He just hit him once and Bazza fell down dead."

The person alleged to have killed Mr Luck left the scene and has not been seen since.

Police are asking the public for assistance in locating this man. He is a large muscular man wearing a dark blue shirt and shorts with distinctive orange-red hair. Nobody reported seeing the car he drove.

Andrew Holmes – Coonabarabran Times

Breakfast in Luanda

Limping as usual, Otto put out his hand to greet Babs. Babs ignored the gesture, gave him a hug and slapped him on the back. "Hello Otto!" Otto wheezed. Babs had not lost his commanding voice or strength. Otto dropped his walking stick and gulped air. "I hope that you had a good flight. Take a seat." The comfortable sofa swallowed the frail German who coughed and caught his breath.

Otto looked up. His face was red. "Guten tag Babs. You say that you have another venture to discuss?"

Babs quickly put a finger to his lips as Jose left the room. The door closed. "We need to heist another aeroplane."

Otto jerked back in surprise. "What?" Their distant profitable relationship had been stable and increasing over the last decade. "Why do you want to do that?" He took off his horn-rimmed glasses and stared at Babs with a myopic gaze.

"Simple Otto. I need turbofan engines for a Boeing 777. The company does not have the resources to buy a new one and there are no used ones on the market. So I thought back to how easy it was to take the 727 and steal those engines. Think of this Otto; if we hijack a 777 and rip off the engines, landing gear and avionics, my problem will be solved and there will be considerable profit to be made!"

"This is a different situation to the 727 isn't it? So what did you have in mind?" Otto was locked on Babs with laser attentiveness.

"Quite simple old friend." Otto winced at the thought of ever being called Babs' friend. "You will find a way to bring two engines intact within six months."

Jose entered still impeccably dressed and quaffed. He did not need instruction. "Coffee to go with your breakfast sir?"

"Ja!"

Babs nodded throwing Jose a provocative glance. Jose blushed.

With great efficiency and little fuss both men had their libations delivered with all the accoutrements. Jose added biscotti to each saucer then bowed and extricated himself walking backward.

Otto handed Babs a little olive velvet purse. "I brought you a gift from Namibia." He handed Babs the purse. "This one is special. It has some special characteristics that remind me of you."

Babs opened the purse and emptied its contents – one 125-carat square cut diamond – he rumbled in mock surprise. "Otto, I didn't think you had the heart!"

"This one is like you: big, bold, impressive but flawed!" Otto laughed at his own joke.

"I also have a gift for you." Babs handed him a manila folder containing a number of articles. "Read the highlighted passages." Babs flicked through his copy. Otto did the same. "While you're eating I can give you a summary of what they contain." He took an egg and a rasher of bacon in one mouthful followed by an orange juice chaser. Otto negotiated with his bagel as to whether the salmon or the onion should surrender first.

"The first article comes from Miami, Florida in the United States of America. It's about an American Airlines crash in Columbia and how outlaw salvagers went in before the authorities. They extracted engine thrust reversers, cockpit avionics and other components from the shattered Boeing 757 and then used helicopters to fly the parts off the steep ridge.

The important comment is that parts illegally salvaged from crashes, counterfeit parts and other substandard components regularly find their way into the world's air fleets often with falsified documents about their origin or composition. Doesn't that sound like the way we have been handling the diamonds since the Kimberly process?"

"Ja." Otto raised his eyebrows and looked at Babs over his glasses.

Babs chuckled. "It goes on to say that a Colombian part trafficker switched to the trade in illegal aircraft parts from drug running. No risk and excellent returns!"

Otto opened his eyes wide leaned back and put his hand to his brow. "You've got to be kidding Babs! I knew that we made a good profit off the old 727, but surely not as much as drug running?"

Babs became animated. "You're half way there." Babs touched Otto's arm. "We sold the whole engines, rather than as individual parts. We could have taken them apart and sold the parts to black market brokers. We got over half a million for each of the engines but if we had disassembled the engines we could have made many times more money than we did. Even in the USA this is a multibillion-dollar illegal economy. Are you with me soldier?"

"Jawhol mein Kommandant!"

Otto sat enjoying his coffee, Blue Mountain from Jamaica. Babs leaned toward Otto. "The next article is from Aviation Week & Space Technology and is only ten days old. It is in your package titled Scarce 777 Parts will Affect Aftermarket."

"I've got it."

Otto looked down his nose at the article. "It says, 'Boeing 777 parts are still scarce. Only 20% of 777 inventories are available from suppliers that are not original equipment manufacturers. This affects price and availability. Aviation Week sees no end to scarcity as only five of the 777s in service have been scrapped'. They–"

Otto leaned forward. "Have you found out pricing for parts from these planes?"

Babs looked up at Otto over his reading glasses. "Yes. I asked Flavio to look into it. You remember he flew you to see me in Angola in 1976?"

Otto sat back and laughed. "Of course I do und that dumb kopf Australian Brian Kelly."

"Well, he brought me impressive figures! The price for a pair of Roll-Royce Trent engines is about $40 million if not more due to shortages. He is still looking for prices of other components. Can you imagine how much each engine would be worth sold as parts?" Babs grinned with an evil twinkle in his bloodshot eyes.

Otto flipped his silver dollar, sat back in the sofa and went for a cigarette. He looked at Babs and thought better. "Let's get a guestimate of the monies we are talking about." Otto looked at the Rembrandt. "Let's decide a mark up of ten. Given the landing gear and avionics and engines we are looking at about quarter of a billion US dollars minus expenses. Hmmm…"

Babs was very pleased with himself. "You can see where I am going? We profited well in 2003, but we have an opportunity to make a killing on a 777. Are you in?" He lit up the room with glinting teeth and outrageous laughter.

Otto sat bolt upright. "Of course! I have nothing better to do at present. I don't like retirement."

"Right. So the next step is for you to come up with a proposal and budget to bring back the most valuable pieces of a 777 for disassembly and resale to part brokers. Okay?"

"Sehr Gut."

"So, when can you put together a preliminary plan for getting me my 777?"

"Let's say a month. I shall rely on you giving me names of crew members flying 777s who can be blackmailed. First I have to determine the route, the airline, the time und so weiter und so forth…" Otto drifted off in thought flipping his coin annoyingly.

"My driver is waiting for you downstairs and he will drive you back to the airport." The meeting was over and nothing would be said until dinner September 18th.

The flight was uneventful. Otto drove home from the airport. He relaxed in a bath to Wagner and the cool evening breeze of the Namibian oasis. He lit a cigarette. Having dried off and dressed in a silk nightgown he took a Windhoek lager and a bottle of Schnapps to the aeroplane room.

It was time to think.

Tom Proposes to Sue

18:20: August 31st 2013 – Kuala Lumpur Malaysia

Tom seemed to have everything going for him. Born in Singapore, he was a popular, determined, intensely focused and well-organised 30-year old. He held the position of Purser with Malaysia Airlines on international long haul flights. He had worked for the company for nine years. His excellent conversational skills and dry sense of humour combined with his well-built, firm body and incredible strength made him irresistible to women. They found him sexy: an attribute that gave 'layovers' another meaning. That is until now. Now he had fallen in love with Li-Juan Zhi known by all as Sue. His life seemed perfect but his worry lines made one suspect that all might not be as perfect as it seems.

Tom Tong was a gambler and he was in over his head.

He shared an old one-bedroom sparsely decorated mould encrusted apartment with Sue, a 31-year old flight attendant. He would do anything for her; even give up gambling. The love he felt for her surpassed the thrill of gambling. There was one problem though. He still owed the loan sharks $15,000 plus interest.

Sue entered the apartment looking tired after a difficult flight with obnoxious passengers. Tom smiled got up and gave her a hug. "Hello honey. How was your day?"

"Not good. We had difficulties with some of the passengers, the planes were overbooked and the flights were late. Sometimes I don't know why I keep this job." Sue was still drop dead gorgeous even in her exhausted state.

Tom's loving eyes undressed her. He stood naked in the bathroom. "How about flying international routes?"

Sue played dumb. "I don't have the seniority do I?"

"Yes, but I pulled some strings to make it happen." Tom told a half-truth as he had only asked on her behalf.

Sue knew he exaggerated. "How did you do that?"

"Let's say I have my ways. Besides you have been flying domestic for six years now."

"And you nine, and were promoted to Purser four years ago after you got the employee of the year award in 2006. I'm sorry that you had to wait for it."

Tom came close to her and kissed the nape of her neck. "Yeah. But now we will fly together on international routes. We will have a chance for many layovers together."

Sue turned around giving Tom a long deep kiss. "I love you Tom Tong."

"And I love you more than life itself." Tom was telling the truth for a change.

Previously, Sue was a photographic model with a Mona Lisa smile: an Asian goddess with incredible sex appeal and an Australian accent. She still looked like a teenager and her slight frame and good looks led others to believe that she was beyond suspicion. Men's jaws hit the ground when they first met her. Her looks could be misleading. She was calculating, focused and goal oriented with exceptional intellect. She was an electronics wiz kid with aspirations to become an authority on quantum mechanics and string theory. She planned on doing a PhD before starting a family. Sue was athletic and surprisingly strong for her slight frame.

Tom asked Sue as he turned on the shower. "Have you heard from your mum recently?"

"Yes. Darwin seems to be having reasonable weather and the veterinary clinic has been busy so her job is not in jeopardy as it was the last time we talked. She's got a new boyfriend! And I talked to dad in the Pilbara in the northwest. He was–" The roar of an airliner taking off interrupted her.

"Where is he now?"

"He's living in Newman and is working at the new Corunna Downs-Klondike mine in Western Australia. Apparently the iron ore is of a higher quality than they expected so his job's not in danger."

Tom got under the spray and soaped his face. "I'll be out in a minute."

Sue had already undressed. She snuck into the shower and squeezed Tom from behind. "What did you say?"

Tom's excitement was showing. "Oh there you are!" Sues eyes lit up. Tom towered above her bent down and kissed her on the head.

"Hold onto that thought big guy!" Sue grabbed his muscly arm and wondered whether his shoulders were as broad as he was tall.

He flinched. "Okay. Scrub my back then I'll do yours – tit for tat."

She washed him all over reaching to shampoo his hair 30 cm above her while the water sprayed over her glistening body. She felt smooth. Her nipples perked up. She was in the mood for more than a shower.

Tom rubbed himself against her, his muscles rippling with anticipation. "Your turn!"

The hiss of the shower stopped. Tom handed Sue a towel.

He lifted her up but she pushed him away. "Not here." She nodded to the bedroom on the other side of the bathroom wall. He was always amazed at her strength – someone so delicate but so strong. Probably her judo expertise helped.

They were still wet when they threw the sheets back and jumped into bed Sue straddling Tom.

Tom grinned. His eyes opened with delight. "Home at last!"

Sue's heart was pounding. "Welcome home honey."

The neighbours were not at home. This was a good thing as they had complained a number of times regarding the noise from the bedroom. Tom and Sue used to giggle in complicity and joked that they must be jealous.

Tom got out of bed. "I'll make dinner tonight."

"Okay. I'll do the washing up," She put on one of Toms oversized T-shirts making her look even smaller.

Sue shook her hair into place. "Tom?"

"Yes."

She came over to him and turned him around and looked him square in the face. "Have you been gambling again?"

Tom felt a nauseating pit opening in his stomach. He thought about how to answer and knew that Sue would see through him if he lied.

He decided to tell the truth. "Yes."

Her eyes narrowed. "How are you doing?"

Tom looked at his feet. "I'm down $15,000."

Sue's hand flew into the air. "What?"

Tom paused and looked up with watery eyes. His chin quivered. "I had a bad streak that's all."

Sue stamped her foot and put he hands on her hips. "That's not all Tom. You've already sold everything you have. When are you going to stop?"

Tom had been thinking about it for sometime now. Somehow it slipped out without rehearsal or ceremony. He mumbled. "When you marry me. Li-Juan Zhi will you marry me?"

Sue frowned and tilted her head. Only then did it sink in. She paused and her face relaxed. A smile rose like the sun breaking through the clouds after a passing storm spreading sunbeams onto the land. She radiated vitality. Her nostrils flared. She felt aroused. "Yes!" She almost, but not quite, forgot about the gambling storm brewing.

Tom was getting up to speed. He didn't miss a beat. His next move was perfectly timed. "When do you want to get married and what about a honeymoon?"

"Only after you stop gambling. I cannot live a life with the losses you are taking." Sue was serious now.

Tom tried to make light of the relationship breaking issue. "I'll make it back." Tom truly believed that this was possible.

Sue was flushed not because of excitement but fury. "That's what they all say. No gambling! Deal?"

Tom could see that continued gambling was impossible. Tom grabbed her and squeezed her tight. "Deal."

She jumped up and wrapped herself around Tom. Tom's towel dropped to the ground. "Also no more women apart from me!"

Tom had a look of mocked surprise. "Of course Sue. I'm a reformed character. You know that.

"You can trust me.

"You are my life."

Operation Vulture

The cuckoo clock struck eight as the familiar sound of the moribund Datsun ceased with a wheeze and a clatter. Cigarette smoke wafted out the front door as Katrina entered. Today, she wore a bright coloured Herero dress and headgear.

Otto was playing with the immense chess set. "Good morning sir! Who's winning Mr von Eschen?" Otto did not answer. He went back to the dinning room table covered with detailed information for the heist of a Boeing 777 and woke his laptop. After about a minute he replied. "Guten Tag Katrina."

"Nice walking stick sir." Otto looked at his new third leg. It had a bright abstract African design.

He did not smile. "Danke."

Katrina feigned interest. "You have been working hard sir. How is your project coming on?"

Otto smirked. "Very well." He was pleased with his research and now he was onto what he liked most: strategy, planning and personnel. He had decided to use Flavio as the pilot and Brian for security again as per Babs' recommendation. "I have a meeting at 10:00. I shall not be home for lunch." He packed up his files, took them to his office and locked the door.

This job was going to be much more complex than the heist a decade before. He now was planning to steal an aeroplane in mid air. What should he do about the passengers?

He met Fritz Schmitz at this office just off Independence Avenue at 10:00 arriving five minutes early. It was another cloudless Windhoek day with a slight breeze wafting the floral scents toward his crooked nose. The noise of the traffic mixed with rumble of the railway felt like home. Fritz's office was on the third floor and there was no lift, so Otto laboured up the flights of stairs. He took a good fifteen minutes to do so. He arrived not out of breath but in obvious pain.

Fritz welcomed him with an open smile getting up to shake Otto's hand and put his hand on his shoulder. "Guten Morgen Otto." Although 55, he had a full head of brown curly hair died so as to hide the few grey hairs that had recently appeared. He was a squat portly man who obviously enjoyed good German wurst and beer. He was happy with his lot in life.

"Well Otto. It's been quite some time hasn't it?"

"Yes Fritz it has. I have an engineering question und I am a little out of date regarding the latest equipment for a project I have been asked to manage. I have to dispose of a large amount of scrap.

Can you tell me what the latest most efficient shredding machine is on the market? I have to shred several tonnes in only a few hours."

"What type of material do you need to shred and to what dimensions?"

'It will be a mixture of aluminium und plastics. The pieces should be no more than 10 square centimetres in size after shredding. The machine must also be able to be moved on a flat bed unless it comes with its own rolling stock."

"Okay Otto. I don't know the best unit off the top of my head. Could I get back to you tomorrow?"

"Absolutely Fritz. I need the information for the day after tomorrow." He handed Fritz a very small burgundy velvet bag. "Here's a little something for your lovely wife."

Fritz opened it and his eyes grew larger. "Heidi will love this! I'll have it set and give it to her on her birthday next week. I'll get you your information tomorrow with no questions asked."

Fritz opened the door and placed a hand on Otto's shoulder. "I'll talk with you tomorrow. Take care old friend."

Otto returned home and got to work.

Otto was concerned about security. All conspirators would have access to all documentation on a secure tablet device. He looked at the six tablet devices still in their packaging and took three, got a knife from the kitchen to cut through the shrink-wrap, then laid them on the table in a row and started each one. It took him about three hours to configure and load the machines with written and graphical material of the proposed heist.

Fritz kept his promise and phoned Otto the next morning, so now he had the final piece to complete the plan. He spent the rest of the day finishing the Avro Lancaster in the aeroplane room.

September 4th came quickly. Following his usual morning routine, Otto put the tablets and his laptop in his briefcase. Now he had to test the plan.

Would they find any holes in it?

The Conspirators

The Land Cruiser had many parking spaces to choose from. Otto chose one without a vehicle on either side. He parked, gave the guard a Namibian dollar coin and hobbled across the street to the Kalahari Sands. Flavio and Brian were still not dressed and were watching cartoons on television. The knock on the door preceded the unmistakable voice of Otto. "Otto von Eschen here!"

The safety chain rattled, released and Brian opened the door. "Good morning sir!" Brian seemed more dishevelled than usual.

Otto looked down his nose at the slovenly two. "This job is far more complex than stealing the 727 in 2003. We are now talking about hijacking an aeroplane full of passengers in mid air. Our task is to review the plan and add to it if necessary."

"Before we start I need to show you how to access your tablet computer." Otto started Babs' computer. He would use this as a demonstration. "Okay boys. Press the large button on the front of the tablet." Flavio and Brian successfully brought life to their machines. Each had a large picture of a Boeing 777 as wallpaper.

"You must take care of these machines. You will not receive paper copies of the plan like last time."

93

Otto took off his glasses and looked at Flavio. "Flavio. Can you fly a 777?"

"Piece of cake Otto. The aeroplane is probably the easiest of all commercial aircraft to fly and can even land itself in an emergency. You just have to adjust the autopilot. The computers do the rest. The autopilot knobs are on the first row of instruments under the windscreen." Flavio pushed his hair out of his eyes. He looked out the window and imagined flying the 777.

Otto laid down the challenge. "Okay. Last time there was no radar to find us. The question is where is the best place to go undetected?" His coin was spinning furiously. "Our job today is to solve these problems und more. The tablet that you have been given contains all the information you will need."

"Our task is to look at the possible places for landing. Where do you think we should land the aeroplane? How do we disassemble it? What do we need und how shall we manage the equipment? How do we salvage without being seen and heard?"

Flavio noted that Otto had no maps of North and South America. "Why have you not included the Americas?"

"The surveillance is unavoidable. We would not be able to escape undetected."

Flavio put up a finger. "That being the case I suggest the we look at areas around the Indian Ocean."

Flavio double clicked the file named runways. The map opened with red dots indicating runways that Otto had marked. He looked up at Otto. "A Boeing 777 is a huge aeroplane and needs a least 1,500 – 2,000 metres of runway to land. It is not like the 727."

Brian had wolfed down his sandwich. Flavio was working on his and Otto's remained untouched. Each sipped their coffee. "Flavio. Don't forget that the aeroplane will have no fuel load and will not need to take off again." Otto looked over the rim of his cup and raised his eyebrows.

Flavio looked at this tablet. "I should be able to land it on 1,300 metres."

"Thanks Flavio. But where would you land it? Obviously, it has to be out of the way und have access for us to bring in the equipment?"

Flavio scratched his head. "We need enough fuel to reach the runway. The best would be to find a flight that is about three quarters of the 777's maximum range. This would give us close to a full fuel load given the required fuel reserve. We could then land it anywhere in one of the hemispheres.

"Boss. We must not forget that the aeroplane is less efficient at lower altitudes and the burn rate of fuel is higher. If I have to initiate avoidance manoeuvres we will use a lot of fuel. I shall have to calculate our range based on fuel consumption at lower altitudes."

Otto cleared his throat. "Good point Flavio!"

Flavio rubbed his right ear. "Somewhere in the Indian Ocean would be best and somewhere within a range of seven to nine hours flying time from a busy airport."

Otto put his finger to his lips and Flavio put up his hand. "The only reasonable match I have found is Indonesia, Borneo, Papua New Guinea und Northwest Australia."

Brain piped in. "My brother lives in a town called Port Hedland in the north of Western Australia. Any good?" Otto became still.

He leaned forward and looked at the map. "Port Hedland was one of my five choices. Brian. Tell me about your brother."

"My brother's name is Bruce. He's a tough bloke. He's up in the area because he had a bar fight that went wrong."

Flavio and Otto leaned forward "What happened?"

"Someone called him carrot top. They shouldn't have done that! Bruce has a real bad temper!" Otto looked at Brian's orange hair and smirked.

Brian sat back, took another drag on his cigarette. "Bruce had his fuse lit and knocked the bloke into oblivion with one punch. He thought he had knocked the guy out but he killed him. It was an accident. Bruce left Coonabarabran in a hurry. He told me that he was going walkabout to avoid the cops.

"Last time we chatted was two weeks ago. He said he was in northern Western Australia around the mines. He works odd jobs and keeps a low profile but he's got a mobile so I can give him a ring."

"Potentially we have someone who could help with the operation und keep his mouth shut? Is that correct Brian?"

Brian's eyes twinkled. "Yes sir! Bruce knows which side of his bread is buttered."

Flavio's eyes opened wide. "I looked at areas where it is possible to keep out of the range of radar. The Indian Ocean is poorly covered. My vote is for the Western Australia route. I used to have a British flight instructor who talked about his stay at Corunna Downs secret WWII airbase near Marble Bar during the war. The Japanese bombed the Aussies mercilessly, but they never found the airbase. They used to fly heavy bombers north and knock the shit out of the Japs."

Otto raised his eyebrows and stretched. "So you're saying that there's an abandoned hidden airfield und the Japanese never found it?"

"Yes sir!"

"Interesting! Gut."

Brian chipped in. "Yeah. What's more it is well within the fuel range you talked about Flavio."

Flavio looked up from the map. Brian had a vacant stare. "Boss. There are a lot of choices within the range that you gave us. I looked for flights taking off from Malaysia, Indonesia, Vietnam and the Philippines. It would be possible to take off from Taiwan, Thailand or China if we have to. I would choose Kuala Lumpur International Airport because it has a large number of 777's flying along flight paths we could manage."

Otto entered 21.4644° S, 119.8472° E into Google Earth and showed the screen to the others. "These are the runways."

"Wow!" Flavio looked closely at the screen. "These are perfect. I hope they are in good condition."

"Okay Brian. It's your turn – the passengers must not know what is happening. We don't want the passengers crashing the aeroplane as they did in Pennsylvania on September 11, 2001! Any suggestions?"

Brian lay on the bed with his eyes closed. "I know what to do about the passengers. We starve them of oxygen until they are dead, and then we repressurise." He sat up with eyes sparkling. "We'll need oxygen of course. Once at the destination we can put the bodies in with the aeroplane bits. What do you think sir?" Otto smiled and rocked in his chair.

Flavio continued. "We can turn off our identification and fly at an altitude between flight levels or 'hit the deck.' That's where we shadow the ground at about 5,000 feet or less."

"Brian. Tell me more about your brother. What's he like?"

"He's my younger brother and he's just turning 50. He lives out of his backpack and works in the Pilbara region as casual labour.

"He's a tall bloke with an attitude and you can see that he has had a rough life. His nose is broken and he has a scar on his forehead he got from falling down drunk when he was 18. He looks a bit like me."

"I think that we should head up the straits of Malacca before heading south clear of Christmas Island's radar, and then come into Australia from the north. We have a problem though. Jindalee over-the-horizon radar network in Australia."

"We don't know much about the Jindalee Operational Radar Network because it's top secret. It reaches up to Indonesia. You will see big areas of coverage north of Australia and to the northwest. We cannot get to our destination without crossing their observation zone."

Brian scratched his cheek. "You told me that radar could only detect an object less than a couple of hundred clicks."

Flavio touched his mouth. "True. This one's different. It is radar bounced off the atmosphere to follow the curve of the earth. It can detect up to 3,000 kilometres away!" He looked up at Otto. "I cannot plot a course that avoids detection by JORN."

Otto put up his hand. "Don't worry! I can tell you JORN is not resourced or tasked to conduct surveillance operations 24-hours-a-day 7-days-a-week. They look for boat refugees coming in from the north rather than old enemies from the northwest."

Flavio looked down at the map and then focused on Otto's coin. "From my evaluation there's only one radar station that we cannot get around and that is the Military installation near Penang."

"I shall talk to Babs about this and get back to you. Anything else?"

"No"

Otto summarised. "We have now confirmed that the flight should originate in Kuala Lumpur then follow Flavio's route und at a time when the radar stations are not manned. We shall handle the passengers by starving them of oxygen und Brian und the other two will confirm they are dead before repressurising the aircraft."

Flavio looked at Otto. "We shall have to deal with the black boxes on the ground as they are in the tail section and can only be accessed from outside." There are two and they are orange not black. They record what the aeroplane is doing mechanically and what is said in the cockpit."

Otto nodded. "The flight data recorder und the cockpit voice recorder."

Flavio looked at Brian and mimed a crash.

"When a crash happens, the black box can play back the conversations in the cockpit and show mechanical details of the aeroplane's activity. It's used for accident investigations."

Otto put his materials and tablet back in his briefcase and unfolded his body from the chair. "I'll see you gentlemen in the morning to complete this exercise."

Flavio and Brian went to Katutura to play with the locals and Otto went home to Sparkle and Wagner.

They now had a plan.

Reuters

Andrew Holmes had kept his job at the Coonabarabran Times because of his mother who had been widowed by the uncompromising steel of a combine harvester. His mother died earlier in the year, so he applied for a position of journalist with Associated Press and Reuters. He had let himself go and was overweight, shoddily dressed and smoked cigars. He could be found most afternoons and evenings at the Royal much to his wife's chagrin.

Andrew arrived late to work on Wednesday. He picked up the mail and guessed the contents of the letter bearing a Reuters return address in Sydney. Andrew ripped open the envelope.

His eyes brightened he stood up straight and focussed on the letter wondering whether it was real. He smiled. It was a small smile of relief and pride. He had job interview in Sydney next Tuesday.

As expected, the interview went well and Andrew was offered a job at the Sydney desk at three times his current salary at the Coonabarabran Times.

He accepted and rapidly climbed to become an international correspondent and moved to the London office.

His first assignment was to investigate Lao Airlines Flight 301, an ATR-72, that crashed shortly before landing at Pakse International Airport in Loas under adverse weather conditions, killing all 44 passengers and 5 crew on board.

London His editor Monty was impressed with his work but not his behaviour.

He worked hard.

He climbed the corporate ladder further and a promotion came following his award winning journalism on the East Timor spying scandal.

The Plan

Otto looked over the rim of his coffee cup as Brian and Flavio sat down. "Flavio. Summarise the plan."

"We will take the night flight MH370 from Kuala Lumpur to Beijing, then hijack the plane as it transfers from Kuala Lumpur air traffic control to Ho Chi Minh City. I'll take over the pilot's job, turn off the aircraft identification and then fly it to Corunna Downs in North Western Australia. To be on the safe side we need an ILS beacon to land. "

"Gut. What else must be done before taking the plane und how many other people do we need for the job?"

Brian scratched his head. "If the passengers have little oxygen they will offer no resistance so I will need a senior flight attendant to run the operation and another to help." He looked at Flavio.

Flavio continued. "Getting oxygen through security will be impossible. We'll have to have the oxygen placed on board by the ground crew and someone to turn off the oxygen to the cockpit. Decompression at 43,000 feet will suck out most of the oxygen giving 10-20 seconds of useful consciousness."

"Gut! What about detection?"

Flavio had done his homework. "All eyes are blind except for the military radar. This could be a big problem. We'll be out of their detection range when we turn south."

"I shall take care of it." Otto looked up from his tablet. "So I need two senior flight attendants for the job then. Any ideas?"

Flavio thought. Brian sat looking at the floor. Flavio nodded and put a finger in the air. He showed his deviant past. "I know quite a few who'd be worth an interview, but only one guy from Malaysia Airlines."

Otto sat up and blew a smoke ring towards Flavio, raised his eyebrows and nodded. "Ja?"

Flavio leaned towards Otto and looked into his effervescent eyes. "He has a dubious reputation. He's a very strong athletic type and a real lady's man. I don't know much more about him, but he has a serious gambling habit and is in debt over his head. He has been avoiding the loan sharks."

Otto grabbed the coin mid air. It rested in Otto's palm. "Excellent work Flavio! Who is he and how can I find him?"

"His name is Tom Tong. Most call him Tom Tom. I don't know his contact information. I would check Malaysia Airlines for that."

Otto had his puppets.

Corunna Downs

10:45: October 29th 2013 – Port Hedland Western Australia

The Australian Outback is an inhospitable arid place – empty, remote, harsh and unforgiving. It covers the majority of the continent and is inhabited by less than 700,000 people. The vast bare open flatness takes your breath away. So will the heat. The Martian soil turns everything red. There is little water. Truly, this alien place requires respect; here nature is the boss.

Within the outback, the Pilbara is a large, dry, thinly populated region in the north of Western Australia. It spreads for 502,000 square kilometres and has a population of 48,600; most people live around the mining areas. It is known to have vast mineral deposits, particularly iron ore. Exporting the ore requires a port: Port Hedland. Port Hedland – named after its founder, Peter Hedland in 1863, now it supports a population of 14,000 and is the highest tonnage port in Australia.

Brian looked forward to seeing his brother Bruce. The 737 from Perth pulled up to the apron and silenced its engines unmasking the sounds of the docks. Otto was first of the three to exit the aeroplane. The wind hit him like a slap in the face with a hot hand.

Otto waited at the base of the stairs for the others. "Wow! I thought that Namibia was hot!"

Brian also was stunned by the blast furnace. "Bruce says that it can get so hot that you can't have a shower until after nine at night because the cold water's too hot!"

Flavio pointed into the distance. "Ooh! Look at the green colour of the water!" Otto dabbed his irritated eyes.

Brian saw his brother waiting. "Hey Bruce!"

"Bloody great to see you mate!" Bruce gave Brian a bear hug.

They held each other's arms. "Still as strong as ever. Keeping out of trouble mate?"

Bruce shrugged his shoulders and bit his lip. "Yeah, pretty much. I just move from place to place with my swag. I've found a place to stay and work for accommodation and food. I'm a bit too old to be a Jackaroo, but I can still keep up with the ankle biters."

"You and kids Bruce? Ya gotta be kidding."

Bruce glared at Brian snarled then relaxed.

Brian cleared his throat. "I can't tell you how good it is to see you mate! Bruce. I want to introduce you to Otto von Eschen." They shook hands and Otto winced as usual.

Flavio didn't wait for an introduction. His curls blew in the breeze. "Hello Bruce. I'm Flavio Ribas." He put out his hand. Bruce took it and shook it vigorously.

Bruce waved away the flies. "Welcome to Australia gents." He opened his arms and made a 360-degree arc.

Brian moved closer to his brother. "He wants to talk with you about a job that will give you lots of money and a place to escape the cops." Brian nodded at Otto.

Bruce looked at Otto. "Where's that?"

"South West Africa –Angola is where you will start and then you can move to wherever you want. It's up to you. I shall make it happen for you if you are interested." Otto watched for clues as to Bruce's intentions.

Bruce looked into Otto's piercing eyes. His orange hair was iridescent in the sun. "Tell me more."

Otto contemplated Bruce's eyes. Bruce seemed as tough as Brian. "Before I tell you anything about this operation you have to know that once you're in you cannot leave except in a body bag!"

Bruce was desperate to solve his predicament. Almost before Otto had finished he blurted out: "I'm in!"

Brian unlocked the rented Toyota Land Cruiser and lifted the bonnet to check the oil and fluids. He retrieved a six-pack of Victoria Bitter aluminium tinnies, known as VB, from the Esky cooler in the boot and put it between him and Flavio in the back seat. "Would you like a beer Otto?"

"Ja!" Otto looked at Bruce's dishevelled appearance.

Bruce slowed for a semi ahead of them. "Boss. This is likely a road train. Watch!" He pulled out to pass.

Otto looked in amazement as they passed five trailers pulled by one semi. "You wouldn't want to meet someone coming the other way!" He pulled out the small notepad from his back pocket and made a note. "This is very good news for bringing equipment in. Potentially we could have three towing vehicles und fifteen trailers. Is that correct?"

"Yes Boss. We would look like any other transport group on these roads."

The vastness of this timeless land was unnerving, especially to those who were used to the claustrophobic closeness of the Angolan jungle. Bruce turned onto highway 138. Otto laid out the plan. Bruce was flabbergasted. "Beauty mate!! You mean that we are going to be a chop shop?"

"If you want to call it that. I prefer the term salvage. Chop shop indicates a criminal activity," as if renaming the activity changed its legality.

Bruce wet his lips. "How do we do the salvage?"

"We shall work out how to get equipment in und aeroplane parts out to the ship without leaving any evidence. Your job will be to manage the salvage und you will report directly to me. We need to work out the details at Corunna Downs."

Bruce saluted Otto. "Bonza mate!"

Otto looked around at the vast horizon. "Bruce. Tell me about the outback. How would you describe it?"

"The outback's vastness and the bare open flatness grabs you and before you realise it, you love it. You can look from horizon to horizon seeing nothing but red dirt, native grasses, mulga wood and eucalypts inedible for sheep or cattle. It has a rare spiritual impact on most. It feels like you are in a place that is the same as it was before humans walked the earth. Rarely do you see another human let alone houses or towns. Most people living in the outback are either part of a mining operation or a station owner."

"What's a station owner Bruce?"

"Just a farmer but on a grand scale. Stations in the Outback are huge and the nearest neighbour is usually hundreds of kilometres away. People stay in touch through satellite phones, Internet and CB radio. Kids get their education long distance through the School of the Air.

In the North during wet season stations can be cut off from the world for months. So the station is a small village in itself, some with greater than 50 people working and living there. The largest working cattle station in the world is larger than Belgium! It's spread out over more than 30,000 km². By comparison America's largest ranch is only roughly 4,000 km². A stockman is someone who works on the station looking after the livestock. A jackaroo is a trainee stockman and a jillaroo is a trainee stockwoman."

"Wunderbar. I need to know more."

"Okay. You will soon experience bushflies. I shall leave that description to you! These pesky nuisances mob you. They land on your exposed skin and clothing to suck up the moisture from your sweat. Then they crawl towards your eyes and mouth. They are the first to greet you in the morning and don't go until evening.

"The sounds you will hear are different from other parts of the world. Depending on where you are, there are many members of the parrot family that can make a deafening row! We might see raucous galahs, cockatoos or corellas on the trip. Also, we might see a 'roo or wallaby too. You need to be real careful with snakes, spiders and other creatures. Treat everything as if it were poisonous and has a lethal bite. Remind me to give instructions for the others when they arrive. The sunrises and sunsets are so beautiful you think you're on another world. No photograph can truly show what it's like. You have to experience a burning red and orange outback sunset to believe it!"

Now it was time for Otto to ask questions about the operation. "What about the Corunna Downs station? Won't they know we are at the airbase?"

"No worries mate! They're selling the place you know." Bruce had done his homework.

Otto nodded. "There's nobody here und we're on the main highway. What happens if you break down on a side road?"

"You meant a track mate! Stay quiet and wait for help. Stay in the shade and drink plenty of water – with no water you die. That's why we have 100 litres of water on board. Talking of water, I need to pay the rent on the beer."

They stopped on the shoulder of the 138 and got out. Bruce started reciting an anthem learnt in school as he relieved himself.

"I love a sunburnt country,
A land of sweeping plains,
Of ragged mountain ranges,
Of droughts and flooding rains.
I love her far horizons,
I love her jewel-sea,
Her beauty and her terror -
The wide brown land for me!"

They had stopped next to a dry riverbed. All was silent except for flies. They swatted these ubiquitous Australian annoyances in what is colloquially known as the 'great Australian salute.' Otto was using his handkerchief to shoo them away. They stuck to his eyes.

The others saluted furiously. "Bloody flies!" Otto and Flavio looked at the red dirt and eucalypts. The trees were quite large for the area. They had a pale multi-coloured bark with olive green leaves.

Flashing lights heralded the first vehicle they had seen for an hour and half. Oversized load in black and yellow adorned the 4 x 4 a Dinky Toy dwarfed by the silence shattering of diesels pulling an excavator occupying both lanes of the road and weighing more than double that of a fully loaded Boeing 747. The kookaburras laughed.

They got back into the vehicle and waited in the air-conditioned cocoon. The convoy passed. "There's a lot of these loads coming down the 138 these days as the Corunna Downs Klondyke mine gets going.

They were at the Marble Bar turnoff. The sign was made of rock: 'Warmest Welcome from Australia's Hottest Town'. Bruce became their tour guide. "Did you know that Marble Bar set a record as the hottest place in Australia when the temperature was over 38.7 degrees centigrade for 160 days straight?"

"No I didn't," responded Otto looking out at a wallaby disappearing on to the distance.

"The slow part now is the track to the airstrip. It will take us a good hour or so to go the 36 kilometres. We'll take the Salgash Road." He turned south. The red dust of the Pilbara followed. It would wait to consume the moving vehicle when once stopped.

Bruce had lost his rear vision. "Keep your eyes out for an oil drum when I call 30 kilometres. The sign to the airbase should be there."

Otto turned toward Bruce. "It looks quite overgrown in places. Can we get heavy equipment in here?" Bruce did not answer immediately as he negotiated a set of potholes. "As long as it is not in 'The Wet'."

Otto rocked slightly out of sync with the vehicle's movement. "What's The Wet Bruce?" Bruce explained it was the time of year when it rained, usually November to April. The skies open in the late afternoon and evenings giving spectacular lightning shows. Then comes the mud and flooding. Creeks swollen into rivers can strand one and the land can suck a truck into the mud. Some vehicles remain bogged for months. "A dry creek bed can go from dry to overflowing instantly. A wall of water sweeps away anything in its path."

Otto took notes. "This could be a problem. It doesn't seem too bad here though." The wheels crunched on the dry dusty gravel.

"Yeah. This area's pretty good. If there is a cyclone then we are in trouble. Otherwise I think we should make it easily it if it doesn't rain too much. We need to prepare for what to do with the equipment if it gets stuck."

Bruce hunched over the wheel. "Have you guys done anything like this before?"

Brian and Flavio looked at each other mischievously. "Yes! We've stolen a 727 ten years ago."

"Where was that?" Brian had never talked about this job before.

Flavio boasted. "Luanda, Angola right under their noses!"

"We only had one problem." Brian's face took on a maniacal appearance. He gleefully looked into his hands remembering the event. "I had to kill the pilot and an engineer."

The scrub fell back revealing one of the runways. The vastness and isolation pleased Otto. No person or any sign of civilisation could be seen or heard.

Otto tapped Bruce's shoulder. "Let's look at the runways." Out they got.

Otto looked for possible onlookers. "How many people visit this site?"

Bruce scratched his head. "I don't know. Probably less than a dozen in a year."

Otto took off his Boer hat and used it as a fan. "Not bad! They seem usable without any preparation! Let's look around."

Brian was after a laugh again. "Watch out for live ammunition, snakes and scorpions. They could really wreck your day!"

Otto stopped waving the flies away and looked at Bruce. "What are we going to do about being seen by people in Marble Bar?"

"I reckon we could wait for a shipment to a mine in Newman and follow them."

Not much was left of the old base. It had been disassembled after it closed in 1946. "Oh! They left the old windsock." Flavio pointed toward a rusty mast.

Flavio dreamed of the place 70 years ago. "I can imagine what it would have been like flying those heavy B-24's – like trying to fly an elephant. My teacher said that he ran out of runway a couple of times and took off on the sand. Imagine 7,000 feet and still not able to take off with four 1,200 horsepower engines. The old Liberators…" he drifted off into his vision of a time gone by.

The sun began to disappear leaving salmon tinted wispy clouds against a cerulean blue sky. It did not give up without a fight until it was snuffed out by the horizon. Without its glow the temperature began to drop and it became still. At long last the flies left them alone.

Brian smiled at Flavio. "Flavio lands the 777 and taxis over to the apron here." Otto pointed to an area clear of vegetation.

"Now what Flavio?"

"I shall shut her down as per the pilot's checklist. Then I disable the power supply and the backup batteries to prevent transmissions, short circuits and fire. Next I'd go for the black boxes in the tail."

"Wunderbar." Otto leant back in his chair with his hands behind his head and his half burnt cigarette hanging from his bottom lip. Do you have any thoughts about the salvage?"

"I'd cut off the tail after Flavio shuts down

the power. It'll make it easier to unload the aeroplane's contents."

Brian grinned. "You mean the bodies don't you mate?" They all groaned.

"What do you need to salvage the aeroplane?"

"A couple of large backhoes and men with plasma cutters, power saws and metal cutters. I would use compressed air for those. I would attach hydrolytic sheers to one backhoe and the other a grappling claw to hold the piece being cut. The claw would also move the scrap leaving the aeroplane clear for further demolition."

"Gut." Otto stretched his aching spine. "How many individuals will you need to salvage the aeroplane?"

"I think that eight might do it. If others were there to chip in it would go faster."

The drive back to Port Hedland was uneventful.

Bruce saw the trio off on their way to Angola.

Closing the Deal

19:00: September 18th 2013 – Klein Windhoek

Otto had difficulty walking up the hill from the car to the restaurant. "Good evening sir." The host greeted him.

"I believe that General Angula made a reservation for us in a private part of the restaurant."

The host nodded. "Actually, he has reserved the whole restaurant for the evening." The host moved into the main part of the restaurant beckoning Otto to follow. "We'll ensure that you have your privacy." He passed an arc over the empty chairs and tables. Otto sat down, crossed his arms and ordered a drink.

The waiter brought the Schnapps and Windhoek lager and then lit the candle in the centre of the round table. The second round arrived but still no Babs. Otto called his mobile and there was no answer. "Surprise!" Babs gave his shoulder a chiropractic squeeze.

Otto recoiled to save his shoulder. "Guten Abend Babs! Wie geht es dir?" He then smirked. "Babs. How is your railroad going these days?"

One of Babs' hobbies was a scale railway that meandered through his estate. He had a number of model engines based on full-sized prototypes. "Wunderbar, as you say. I am extending the track and building a tunnel behind the pool keeper's house. How are the model planes coming along?"

"Not very well. I am still working on the Liberator. Most of my time I have worked on the 777 question."

"Excellent! But sorry for the delay – poor Liberator." Babs wiped an imaginary tear from his cheek.

Otto opened his mouth to speak but Babs put up his hand.

"Nathan… hmmm… Did you see Nathan Goldstein yet? Has he given you the operating funds for the job?" Nathan Goldstein managed Babs' accounts and kept two sets of books.

Otto rubbed his knee. "Yes. I saw him at the Kalahari Sands when Flavio and Brian were down for a briefing. I have arranged for a meeting with him in Washington to deal with the details and sign the required papers. I'll keep you posted."

Babs' face relaxed. "How are those two?"

"They are quite the comedians and now we have Bruce, Brian's brother as part of the team. He is much more on the ball than Brian and naturally took command of 'operations' when we visited the site."

"What and where is Carooo Downs?" Babs put his hands on his thighs thrusting his elbows forward.

"Corunna Downs is the perfect place for us. You won't believe it. It's in the north of Western Australia."

"I need staff on the 777 to manage the passengers und take the aeroplane. Flavio mentioned a purser who may be an asset. I think he can be controlled. His name is Tom Tong und he works for Malaysia Airlines. Apparently he is a gambler und the loan sharks are threatening bodily harm. Do you have a contact that can vet him?"

"I'll take care of it. So you're saying that it will only take four people to get the job done?"

Otto fiddled with his tie. "Yes. That's for the airborne portion of the job. I need to nail down Tom Tong or his equivalent und another flight attendant.

"We need a crew to demolish the plane. Skills required are: welding, plasma torch use, electrical engineer, truck driver, backhoe operators and mechanic. I need two or more unskilled loyal and hard working labourers. All men should be stronger and fitter than their local soccer team. All personnel must be motivated and will work with others in the gang and must be able to work at maximum physical effort for 24 hours at least."

Babs ran his tongue along his teeth pushing out his cheek. Otto followed its movement as if it were a clue as to what Babs was thinking. "I can do that."

A new burst of aroma followed the waiter. "Would you like some wine with the your food sir?"

"Yes. I'll leave the choice up to you." Babs grinned showing off his new gold filling in his front tooth balancing the one he commissioned some nearly four decades previously.

Babs adjusted his Gerry Garcia tie. "You were telling me about this Tong who is a Purser, correct?"

"He's a gambler und has clocked up a debt he can't handle. I still need to meet him. He'll be on his honeymoon in Vietnam in December. His new wife is also a flight attendant on international flights."

Babs looked at his watch. "Why don't you go to Vietnam and interview them. If they are what you need then I shall make sure that the gambling debt disappears. But he must know that I am holding his debt and will not collect from him if the heist is a success. If not – you know what happens."

"We are looking at a flight going from Kuala Lumpur to Beijing. The route seems the best as it fits the time of day und fuel requirements. The heist would occur during the time of 'hand off' from Malaysian air traffic control to Vietnam. We only have one problem concerning invisibility: Malaysian Military radar."

"I'll take care of it."

Otto sighed. "Danke schoen."

Babs straightened and looked at the tablet. "What about the black box?"

"It goes to a deep watery grave on its way back to Angola."

Babs put his fingers together in a steeple under his chin. "What about fuel?"

"There's more than enough. I think we shall have to dump at sea when coming into Australia."

Babs moved closer. "How will you dispose of the bodies?"

Otto waited with an artificial pause. "They will be in the discarded shipping containers with the shredded materials."

Babs bought the best champagne that Am Weinberg's had, a Tête de Cuvée. They exchanged pleasantries and went their separate ways.

Tom's Gambling Debt

Tom went to the Casino to win back his losses and make some money for his honeymoon in Vietnam: he and Sue were booked on an early morning flight as passengers. Smoke filled the dimly lit room. A puddle of light reflected the glint of the spinning Roulette wheel – Roulette was Tom's downfall.

Tom forced a smile and faint beads of perspiration appeared on his top lip. He wiped them off, looked around then focused on the wheel; its power over him was total. He looked at his stash noting it had grown. He should get out now while ahead but the wheel had him.

Two burly bouncers approached Tom. "Mr Big would like to see you Mr Tong." Mr Big was the gentleman who had loaned him $15,000 some time ago. He was a loan shark, a shark hungry for repayment.

Tom entered a room on the second floor, the room where he had originally met Mr Big for the loan. Mr Big had a smooth but serious voice. "Selamat malam Mr Tong."

"Selamat malam Mr Big." Tom dared not enquire as to his real name. He could only make out the glowing tip of his cigar. The rest was hidden in the shadows.

Mr Big leaned forward enough to reveal the tip of his nose in the light. Tom squinted trying to make out his features. "I believe that we had an agreement that I would loan you money and you would pay me back with interest – correct?"

Tom grew pale. "Yes."

"I'm wondering where my money is. You have had it for a long time so now you must repay." He waived his cigar showing his chubby hand in the light. "Let me refresh your memory. I loaned you $20,000 back on the first of August didn't I?"

Fear gnawed at Tom's stomach. "Yes sir." He felt a brick in his chest and his left jaw went into spasm. It suddenly dawned on Tom that he might not be able to talk himself out of this meeting. He had managed to escape the last three monthly requests for payment. "So I need to get the $20,000 back to you soon."

"Tonight plus interest! I gave you an introductory rate of 12% rather than 20% per week. This was a reward for you initial prompt partial repayment, but the rest has remained unpaid for 18 weeks, so the interest and principal would be–" he paused while Mr White pulled out a black book from the briefcase on the table. He thumbed the pages until he found it. "Ah yes here it is, Mr Tom Tong loan of $40,000 for one week. Next line Mr Tom Tong repays $5,000 leaving $39,000 left to pay. The mathematics is this Mr Tong. $40,000 plus $8,000 interest minus the repayment of $5,000 gives us $43,000, correct?"

"Correct." Blood rushed through Tom's ringing ears.

"No payment has been received since then leaving 18 weeks of interest at 12% compounded weekly plus the principal meaning that you now owe me $370,348.75 as of today."

Tom nearly fell off the chair. He turned ashen white.

"I shall give you 'til midnight to pay me back."

"I shall get it to you later tonight. I'm on a winning streak at present."

By midnight he lost everything.

Mr Black was next to him when his gamble of $30,000 evaporated. "Come with me." Mr Black grabbed the prisoner by the collar. "We have an appointment with the enforcer."

Tom shook uncontrollably while the other gamblers looked on. He craned his neck to look at Mr Black. "What's the enforcer?"

Mr Black held Tom's arm in a vice grip. "You'll see." He marched Tom through the back and downstairs to the storeroom. Under the single swinging light bulb was a blacksmith's hammer and anvil.

Mr Big was in the shadows but Tom could see his crossed legs dressed in custom made Italian slacks. He moved his free foot as if to music. "I'm really sorry to have to do this before your wedding day. As an act of generosity I shall use the little finger on the right hand. Your ring finger will be untouched and you can hide the other hand in some manner. Now before we start, any questions?"

Tom looked at the anvil, the hammer and lastly his finger. "Yes! Can we wait until I get back from the wedding?"

"No. Mr Black and Mr White you know what to do." The glowing tip of the cigar nodded.

Tom tried to resist but it was futile. Mr Black held Tom in a half Nelson while Mr White placed his right hand on the anvil. "Mr Tong. Please listen. If you move I will break your hand." With that he picked up the hammer and swung hard.

The anvil did not ring under the blow as Tom's smallest finger was smashed beyond recognition. Blood and bone chips splattered the walls. His nail was somewhere on the floor. Mr White went over to the rusty old sink and washed the hammer and returned with bandages. He delicately bandaged the devastated digit.

Mr Big seemed energised by the event. "You see Mr Tong, I mean business. Now go and enjoy your wedding and I shall collect from you when you return.

Tom nodded stunned and then the pain hit him.

Tom went home and turned the key in the lock of the apartment and the smell of the evening meal greeted him. Sue sat up in bed waiting. "You're late honey. Come here and give me a kiss. What's a girl got to do for a little–" She saw his bandaged finger soaked with blood. Her eyes widen and her mouth dropped open.

Tom shivered even though the apartment was about 30 degrees. "Could you get me some aspirin honey? I have something to tell you."

She returned from the bathroom with the tablets and glass of water. "Here you are. Go on."

"I was trying to win the money back and–"

Sue cracked her knuckles and furrowed her brow. Her eyes caught fire. "Tom. You know what I think of gambling! I cannot believe that you went to the casino again! I should walk out of here right now." She slammed the cupboard door. "You broke your promise!"

Tom tried to put on a brave face but the pain brought tears to his eyes. "I can explain." He took a deep breath straightened his back and looked at Sue straight in the eyes. "I went to the casino to try and settle my debt with the loans people. I owe $370K." Tom was barely audible. He waited for the response and cringed.

Sue moved back and raised her voice. "What are you going to do? We can't cancel the honeymoon! It's already paid for and so is the wedding!" She moved away from Tom and looked out the window.

"One thing I promise you in all sincerity honey: I will never gamble again." He sat down, bent over and wept.

Sue moved toward the door then looked around the apartment. She could have taken the easy way out but decided that Tom was worth fighting for. "Tom. I will always love you and I'll do all that I can to help you, but this is your responsibility. If you fail at this then I would say our marriage is doomed from the beginning."

Sue opened the medical kit and started undoing the bandage. "The question is how are we going to get the money?"

"I just don't know."

Christmas Day at Manny's

07:30: December 25th 2013 – Melbourne Australia

Manny's Milk Bar was closed and would remain so all day. This was the only day off in the year for the Liu family. Decorated with Christmas ornaments hanging from the dusty flickering fluorescent lights, the store shouted the celebration to those looking in from outside. A Christmas tree flashed in the window and a crèche was on the table where regulars usually drink their tea. Christmas carols drowned out the hum of the refrigerators.

It was early. "Look at what Santa brought me!" Li-Li jumped onto the bed landing between Li-Na and Manny.

Manny gave her a big kiss then lifted her over to Li-Na. "Happy Christmas angel!"

"I'll check on Li-Li while you make us something suitable for Christmas." Mrs Liu was sitting in the living room knitting. "Happy Christmas mother!"

"Happy Christmas son." Mrs Liu really didn't celebrate Christmas. She preferred celebrating the Chinese New Year. Nevertheless she played her part for Li-Li's sake. "Do you want me to help you get ready for the beach?"

"I'll get the stuff ready for the family. You'll need to bring a bathing suit. I'll take a towel for you. I am sure it is hot enough to swim and the waves will be small."

Mrs Liu put down her knitting and looked up at Manny. "Very good."

Li-Na called Li-Li. "You have a special present from your grandmamma and grandbaba! Here it is angel!" Li-Na handed the present wrapped in Chinese decorative paper to Li-Li.

Li-Li tore open the package. There it was; a rag doll handmade by her grandmother. "Oh he's cosy!" Li-Li held him close and snuffled his rag hair. "I'm going to call him Mr Snuggles. He's a boy and I'm a girl. We can play can't we dad?"

Manny reached down to give Li-Li a hug. "You can bring him and leave him in the car while we go to the beach."

"I want to take him to the beach!" Li-Li kicked the dresser and pouted.

Li-Na was not going to deal with tantrums on Christmas day. "If you make a fuss I shall put Mr Snuggles away."

Li-Li upped the ante. "He's mine and I am going to snuggle him wherever I go!" She stamped her foot.

"All righty then. If you lose him I can't get another one. Grandmamma made it." Li-Li crossed her arms and looked away.

She capitulated. Li-Li looked down. "Okay, I'll leave him in the car."

The Honeymoon is Over

Tom Tong lay awake watching the reflections of the dawn bounce off the ceiling fan. The pulses of light were rhythmical, predictable and soothing. If only the roulette wheel had been as predictable. His newly minted wedding ring caught the sunlight. He looked around the room and saw the empty bottles of exotic juices, a tea set and the decimated bowl of fruit. He smiled. This was a wonderful place to be. Tom's playboy days were over; he had just married the love of his life. He rolled over and caressed her neck, nibbling her awake. "Good morning honey. Did you sleep well?"

Still surfacing from the depths of sleep, she turned around and smiled. "Yes. This has been the highlight of the honeymoon. It's a pity that we have to go home tomorrow." She threw her leg over Tom. She lifted herself arching her back and kissed Tom on the lips. "Let's go and have breakfast by the pool?"

"Of course we can, but…" he responded to her kiss "…maybe later when…" she melted as she slumped back supine into the perfect mattress.

Sue started to rub his chest. "Just be quiet and enjoy the moment!" The sight of her perfect body made him forget all his woes but did not dampen the pain from his crushed finger. He looked at

131

the bandage then smiled thinking that he was the luckiest man on the planet with her by his side. He kissed her gently, ever so gently, fully aware of his turgid maleness. She giggled and in return lightly bit his left nipple, not too lightly, strong enough to get an alarmed response. They laughed. Their appetite for each other replaced the need for food. They gazed dreamily into each others eyes unblinking then kissed again, again and again. Sue was becoming flushed and her breasts swelled under his touch. She moaned slightly with excitement. She held him. "What are you going to do about that big guy?" The challenge was given. Tom accepted.

The pool by the beach was one of two at the Evason Ana Mandara Nha Trang in Nha Trang, Vietnam. It was crystal clear and seemed to meet the sea, an illusion carefully designed to match the mountain backed beachfront strip. The resort was impeccably kept. Staff was trained to satiate a visitor's every desire. Unfortunately tomorrow was the time to return home to Kuala Lumpur and face Mr Big.

A frail senior citizen using a walking stick approached.

Tom shivered even though the temperature had passed thirty degrees. Had Mr Big sent the stranger? "Excuse me sir. Can I help you?"

Otto wore a crooked smile. "Do you mind if I sit with you for a while?" Otto mesmerised Tom with his piercing stare. "I have a business proposition for both of you: Tom Tong und Li-Juan Zhi, correct?"

"Call me Sue. Who gives me the pleasure of this meeting?"

Otto flexed his bad knee. "My name is Otto von Eschen."

"Look. We are on the last day of our honeymoon and business is the last thing on our minds."

Otto emitted cold blue fire from his eyes. "Tomorrow you are going to have to deal with a rather significant gambling debt, nicht wahr?"

Tom and Sue turned to each other. "What do you want from us?" Sue was not intimidated by Otto's stare.

Otto looked at her and recognized her good looks. "Quite simple." He put down his briefcase. He paused to pull out his silver dollar. Otto baited the trap. "I shall pay your debt in full if you work on a job for me."

Tom's eyes grew wider. "What's the job?"

"I can't tell you unless you both agree to the deal. Once you have there is no going back. Failure is not an option und will have fatal consequences!"

Tom pursed his lips, scratched his head and looked out to sea. "We don't have much of a choice do we?" Sue put out her hand to comfort him.

"Not really." Otto stopped and looked at them closely. "Upon successful completion of the job you will be paid an additional $250,000. If you accept you will not have to worry about bodily harm upon your return tomorrow and will have more money in your account than you would ever earn in a year. Any questions?" Otto sat there with a synthetic smile and raised eyebrows.

Sue held onto Tom as if to protect them both. "Do I have a role?"

"You're ahead of me! Yes you do und it is essential that you also agree to the deal as an active partner. I shall pay you $250,000 for your help in this project. So together you walk away with a future ahead of you." Otto jutted his head forward waiting for an answer.

Sue had a million questions race through her mind. "Where will we live?"

"Angola."

"Oh." They looked at each other and frowned. They both spoke as one. "Where's Angola?"

Otto lit another cigarette. "It's on the west coast of Africa above Namibia. You'll be given new identities und free accommodation for as long as you are resident of Angola. I cannot guarantee your safety in other countries."

Otto held his hand out to Sue. "Deal?"

"I agree," She said a little too quickly for Tom's comfort.

Otto held his hand out to Tom. "Deal?"

"Deal."

Otto put down the laptop and opened his briefcase. Otto pulled out two personnel binders.

"Okay. Let's begin. You are both flight attendants, nicht wahr?"

"Yes we are." Tom scratched his head. "What's nicked-var mean?"

"Sorry, it's German for 'not so?' or 'correct.' Tom it is my understanding that you are now a Purser working for Malaysia Airlines on the overseas flights, nicht... correct?" Tom nodded. "And you Sue are also a flight attendant working on long haul flights?"

"Yes."

I understand that Sue 'was charged but not convicted of forcible confinement when she used GBH, known as the date rape drug, to nobble the competition!' Apparently the model competition went to you as the number one contestant had fallen."

"I'm afraid so. I was so young and wanted so much to—"

"You never told me!" Tom became still. His jaw was fixed. He looked through her but she did not flinch.

"Enough kinder!" Otto contemplated the file and gloated. These two will work together and carry the show through no matter what the consequences.

"My client needs spare parts from a Boeing 777 to keep his machines aloft. One of the three 777s has been grounded due to an engine failure. These machines cost every minute they are employed by an airline. He needs an engine for the plane as without revenue an aircraft on ground can push a financially insecure company into bankruptcy. There is currently a shortage of 777 parts. We are going to steal a Boeing 777 und cut it up for its most lucrative parts."

Otto looked at Sue. "I need you to drug the pilot und starve the passengers of oxygen. It will be during the night after the first service. You will have supplemental oxygen; the passengers und crew will not. Otto looked up.

"Tom, as you will be the Purser on the flight, you will be in charge of the operation while in the air. There will be two others as part of the team: Flavio Ribas our pilot und Brian Kelly a mercenary. Brian will help you with the passengers und will handle any unsavoury matters."

Tom was alarmed by the thought that they might be asked to physically kill someone. "Does that mean that Brian will take care of passengers that might be still alive?"

"Ja. That's his specialty. You only have to make sure that the lack of oxygen has done its job. I know this is hard, but you will have to check the pulse of each passenger. Let Brian know of anyone that has a pulse und he will take care of the situation.

"Li-Juan. I need you to bone up on the avionics of this airplane. You will work in the electronic and equipment bay to disable certain modules und confirm that oxygen will not reach the pilot's masks.

Otto straightened his back. "One more thing. I shall need your help with the bodies. You are strong Tom. I am sure that you will be able to help unload them when we land?" Tom nodded then looked at the ground.

Otto stopped flipping his coin to light another cigarette. "I have a little wedding gift for you." Otto pulled out a small velvet black purse. "Please put out your hand Li-Juan." She did and Otto poured the contents of the purse in to her open hand.

Sue's eyes grew bigger. "Wow! I have not seen such a large diamond in my life!" Tom sat quietly and did not comment.

"Tom, I warn you that if you are caught gambling again you will be terminated. Do I make myself clear?" Sue reeled back as if the word terminate had been a bullet passing through her heart.

"Yes. I have already vowed to Sue that I shall not gamble."

"Gut! I shall be in touch." The meeting was at an end.

The honeymoon was over.

Boeing

"Today we will see how they build a 777 at the Boeing plant in Everett. We shall be going on the tour just to see the airplane up close und see the size of the task ahead. Tomorrow we fly to California to the Mojave Desert to watch the demolition of a retired 747."

Flavio headed the black Suburban towards Mukilteo, some 25 miles north of Seattle, being careful not to exceed the 60-mile per hour speed limit. They reached Everett the home of Boeing producing 747, 767, 777 and 787 Dreamliners and Brian's mouth dropped open. "Holy crow! Look at that building! I've never seen one so big!"

Flavio tried to show Otto that he had done his homework. "Believe it or not, that building is bigger than Disneyland and is six stories high. The side with the mural is the largest mural in the world."

They obtained permission for Otto to take the tour for the mobility challenged as there was no way that Otto would have managed the walking needed for the main tour. The tour began and they saw how a 777 was built.

A Boeing 777 is a huge aircraft 209 feet long, 61 feet high and has a wingspan of 212.7 feet. It has a maximum flight range of over 9,000 nautical miles at a cruise speed of 557 miles per hour at an altitude of 35,000 feet. Depending on its configuration it seats from 301 to 440 people and takes 45,220 gallons of fuel and weighs up to 656,000 lbs.

Flavio said. "I noticed that they have different engines depending on the model: Rolls Royce or GE. The engines are larger than I thought and are wider than a normal semi."

Brian slept well after watching two movies on HBO while Flavio spent his evening going through flight plans and radar points.

He was ready to fly MH370.

Yearning

The Milk Bar was empty. Manny was swimming in receipts and cash register tapes organising them for Mrs Liu. Li-Na was stocking the shelves. She sighed and dropped her shoulders. How she yearned to hug her parents.

"All righty then. Let's look and see whether we have the money for a holiday in China." Manny knew that this was a financial impossibility, as he could not leave his mother and Manny's Milk Bar to travel with them, even if they could afford it. He did not want to send Li-Na and Li-Li alone.

"It would be excellent for Li-Li to spend time with your parents and good for them too." Li-Na put down the can of soup, blinked and looked up at Manny.

"I love you Manny, you silly sausage."

The Boneyards

"Today we fly to Los Angeles und drive up to Mojave Air and Space Port. It's also called the Civilian Aerospace Test Center. We will visit the boneyards to watch how they recycle old aircraft."

The early morning shadows heralded another warm and dry day in the Mojave Desert. A cloudless sky greeted the troop as they saw the boneyards from a distance. As they got closer they could see faded tails stretching to the horizon. Otto asked, "Flavio. What can you tell us about the boneyards?"

"Here's a summary." Flavio looked at his handwritten notes in his folder. "When airliners reach 20 to 25 years they are at the end of their service life. They make their last flight to places like Mojave to be stored and stripped of their parts or sold. Scrap companies buy the old airframes and drag them to a remote corner of the airport to chop them up and shred them."

"Exactly Flavio. We are about to see the salvage of a 747." Otto gave a crisp nod. "We'll use the same technique on the 777."

They were met at the gate by identical twins, Jose and Marco Fernadez. "Buenos días Mr. von Eschen!" Jose gave Otto his hand. Otto shook it and passed him a thick envelope.

"Gracias senior von Eschen!" He stuffed the envelope in his overalls. "Have a look around first, then we'll go and show you how easy it is to scrap a jumbo."

The ghosts in the boneyard reached out to them. A desert breeze banged and scraped loose metal and old doors as the airplanes groaned and sighed settling onto their tire rims under the desert sun bleeding the last of their hydraulic fluid into the sand.

"Over this way." The squat 265 pound 5' 5" Jose pointed toward a large excavator sitting next to a 747. The airplane did not have engines or undercarriage. Marco mounted the excavator and with a belch of black smoke and diesel roar, the excavators attacked the hulk.

Flavio pointed to the jaw at the end of the excavator. "What's that thing on the end of it? It's not a scoop?"

Jose pointed to the excavator. "That's what they call 'the anvil.' It's really a giant hydraulic metal sheer. Just watch!" In no time Marco had cut off the tail.

Brian put his hand to his mouth. "Wow! It goes through the airplane like a hot knife through plastic!"

Otto seemed pleased with Brian's reaction. "I thought that you would be impressed." He put on his sunglasses.

Brian rubbed his jaw. "I see where this fits into the plan. Bruce's job will be to make sure that it is done right, correct?"

Otto raise is eyebrows and focused his gaze. "Ja. Bruce is the foreman for the job und will be the boss for the workers. I'll be there with you if you have questions while we gut und cut up the airplane."

Another crash and the sound of tortured metal got their attention. Marco had cut through a wing. In less than half an hour he had cut off the wings, nose and tail. He then cut the wings in two and the remaining fuselage into three sections. The whole operation took just 45 minutes.

The excavator fell silent and Jose led them to a giant shredder some 75 yards away. Here other excavators fitted with claws lifted the bones of the carcasses and unceremoniously dropped them into the large hopper. After shredding, all that remained of the airplane was a container full of glittering aluminum pieces none being larger than a tennis ball.

Brian slapped his hand on his forehead. "Christ! That's bloody unreal!"

Otto stopped. "Jose! Marco! Danke schoen – Wunderbar. Can I get a lift back to the truck?"

"Si senior. I will get Pedro's vehicle."

The Heist

Chapter 1 - Bao-Yu Gao

Ming Gao woke at six and turned to Bao-Yu sleeping restlessly next to him. He breathed in her ear, hoping to wake her gently. She responded with a cough. "Lao-gong. I can't breathe," she gasped.

"Why don't you sit up while I put on some tea?" He deflated. "Maybe later on we can go for a breath of fresh air, or should I say the best air Beijing has to offer?" She made an effort to smile.

"I would like that. The sun's shining!" She looked at the blood red sun in the anaemic grey sky. "I'll feel better after I get up, I'm sure." She looked weak. She had been sick for much more than a week.

The dark rings under her smiling eyes distressed Ming. "Perhaps we should go to the hospital Lao-po?"

"Not now. I'm too tired. Tomorrow."

Ming should have insisted.

Nathan Goldstein

Otto was meeting Nathan Goldstein for a financial matter, a meeting to be held in the presidential suite of the JW Marriott a couple of blocks from the White House. He entered the suite and half smiled at the opulence. He put his briefcase on the large cherry wood dining room table.

Otto had slept well. The presidential suite was more like an apartment or small house than a hotel room. There were signed portraits of past Presidents of the United States who had rested their weary heads in the bed he arose from. Otto relaxed in one of the sumptuous leather armchairs and checked the time. It was now 15:07. He was expecting Nathan Goldstein at 15:30.

Otto sat at the table drumming his usable fingers waiting for the knock. He let in Nathan and gave him a sideways glance. "Guten tag Nathan." Nathan avoided eye contact, turned and took off his black fedora and coat.

He laid out two binders and slid one over to Otto. Next he placed a small scale between them and then retrieved a stack of wrapped Ben Franklins from his briefcase. Finally he retrieved a black notebook.

"Show me the diamonds." Nathan retrieved a jeweller's loupe.

Otto passed him the box.

Nathan spent the next two hours classifying the diamonds into groups of similar color and clarity and then weighed each pile then tapped the results into his calculator. He pushed the pile of 100-dollar bills over to Otto and raised his eyebrows. "Here is some spending money from Mr. Angula."

Otto pulled the pile of notes closer to him. "Danke schoen."

"We need the equipment shipped to Port Hedland in Australia. You will take care of the responsibility of ensuring the equipment gets there. Here's the list." Otto slid a single sheet of A4 paper across the table. "We shall be coming on a ship from Hong Kong with the equipment. It is essential that the equipment arrive on dry land in Port Hedland on March 7th! There should be enough diamonds to cover the cost."

Nathan picked up the list while Otto gave the details. "Our heavy equipment is two Truck cranes Demag AC200-1, two Cat backhoes M325D-LMH, a Cat front end loader CAT 450F, a trail behind Generator CAT XQ300, a Portable air compressor Sullair 900H, BTI hydraulic sheers SH50R and Weima metal Shredder WLK 20 and a Kenworth W900 semitrailer. We also need nine containers and rolling stock and 20 forty-four gallon drums." Otto gave him a file with sales brochures.

Nathan took the brochures. "Okay."

Nathan retrieved a pile of legal sized documents. "Mr. von Eschen. Here are the papers that you need to sign on behalf of Mr. Angula. I am sorry that you had to come all this way."

Otto signed the papers.

Nathan picked up an apple from the fruit basket. "I did some rough calculations and there should be more than enough diamonds to cover the purchases. I'll call you on your cell if there is a problem. If you have problems send me a text."

"I look forward to confirmation that the equipment und transport are on track." Otto opened the door.

"Viel Glück!"

At the Hospital

Bao-Yu's coughing was worse and now she slept propped up with a pillow. Her skin was a purple-blue tone. "Lao-po, I can't see you like this. Let's get dressed and go to the hospital." Ming covered his eyes.

"Give me a moment – I can't breathe." She coughed and finally she brought up a little foam.

Ming waited and looked around the small apartment that they called home since downsizing once Li-Na emigrated. He saw the evidence of a rich and well lived life. Among the hangings were photographs of Li-Na and Li-Li. The kitchen is where paintings done by Li-Li hung.

They took a taxi to the Beijing United Family hospital, in the Chaoyang District of Beijing. "We'll be there soon Lao-po and I am sure they can find out why you are having trouble breathing."

As they passed through the automatic doors, the acrid smell of Beijing transformed into antiseptic scents of the hospital. Triage immediately sent Bao-Yu to the Cardiovascular Centre known for handling high-risk cases of heart disease.

Dr Yap marched into the room and closed the privacy curtains. "Good morning, I am Dr Yap. I am a cardiovascular specialist." He continued reading the initial clinical examination by the

149

resident, results of blood taken upon arrival and the ECG.

He motioned Ming to step outside with him. "Professor Gao, your wife's heart is very sick. I wish that you had come in earlier, as there is little we can do."

"Is she going to die?"

"Yes."

The comment hit hard. "How long?"

"It could be at any time but probably a month or two. She is very unlikely to reach her next birthday."

The X-ray, ECG and other tests confirmed Dr Yap's diagnosis – end stage congestive heart failure.

Dr Yap antiseptically pulled out a prescription pad from his white coat pocket. "You'll need to get this prescription filled. It is important that these tablets be taken at the same time each day. You might also try Chinese tonic herbalism."

The nurse came back in with some tablets in a small cup. She gave them to Bao-Yu with a glass of water. "Once you have taken your medicine, you can get dressed and go. You will have to stop at Admissions to fill in some paperwork before you leave the building." Ming didn't quite know what to say or do.

Bao-Yu the dynamo's light was dimming.

Fare Skye Departs Hong Kong

The tug waited for the Fare Skye to finish loading. She was an 80,000-tonne cargo vessel about to leave the port of Hong Kong carrying a mixture of containers and heavy equipment including the Angula shipment. From the vast sky-blue painted hull to the 12 hulking pistons deep in the engine room she was immense. Three massive gantry cranes whirled back and forth like War of the Worlds robots as they lifted and organised 12 metre sea containers and heavy equipment into its colossal hold like a mother picking up her child's toys.

Captain Charles Jones, known as CJ, was a seasoned mariner of 31 years with a Manchester accent. He was a slim tall man with sea blue eyes, long salt and pepper hair with a tint of red and a full beard.

He was on the bridge sipping coffee while overseeing the cast off from Hong Kong. Otto entered the bridge. The captain glanced at Otto and smiled.

Otto wrinkled his nose. "Captain?"

"Yes, Mr von Eschen." CJ did not look away from the task at hand.

Otto made small talk "How do you ensure the cargo is safe?"

The captain turned to Otto with furrowed brow and a determined jaw. He had a pleasant baritone voice. "All cargo is tied down and heavy equipment is lashed to the ship with steel cables and tightened with turnbuckles. Interlocking cones keep the containers locked together and the crew ensures that the equipment is lashed down and secure a number of times each day."

Captain Jones had worked his way up from the wharf to deckhand and then onto the merchant shipping line to eventually become a commissioned captain. His name was legendary to some, as previously his dead reckoning had saved his ship and crew from running aground when the ships' electrical system failed during a storm.

A tug pulled the Fare Skye into navigable mill pond waters leaving the smell of creosote and rotten fish behind. The deep rumble of the engines was interrupted by a deafening blast from Fare Skye's horn. Soon they headed across a hyaline sea into the sunset, over the horizon to Port Hedland.

Otto's team occupied most of the 'tourist' space on the ship. Otto had purchased all of the rooms even though two were vacant. Tom and Sue and Brian and Flavio would occupy the vacant rooms on the return trip.

The sun was over the yardarm and it was time for dinner. The mess was configured with four tables placed together. Otto and the team sat down with the captain and his wife, the chief engineer and first officer and other officers at appointed seating positions. The smell of shepherd's pie was irresistible, so the introductions were short.

The gang met after dinner. "My name is Otto von Eschen und I am the manager of operation Vulture; Vulture Base is Corunna Downs and MH370 the Albatross." Carlos handed out the binders. "You will be expected to memorise und understand the information in your package. We'll meet after dinner each evening to go through the details of the plan. The rest of the time is yours to enjoy. Bruce Kelly will be the foreman at Corunna Downs but in the interim Carlos is my second in command." He nodded to Carlos.

Carlos's brown eyes sparkled. "Okay men. Lets get on with introductions. You already know Otto. My name is Carlos Amado. I am an electrical engineer and my primary job will be to help decommission the electronics and equipment."

He pointed to Adrien to the left of him.

"My name is Adrien Rafael. I'm a heavy machinery operator. I shall drive and operate one of the cranes and will run the anvil, the large metal cutter on one of the excavators."

"Next."

"I'm Geraldo da Costa and I shall be driving a crane and will operate the other excavator fitted with the grappling claw." He rushed his words and looked down shyly.

Carlos thanked him. "Obrigado."

"Next."

"I'm Nelson Xitu and I am a certified welder and have considerable experience."

Carlos pointed to Miguel.

"Miguel Flores. I am a general labourer and will operate the shredder." He looked at each member of the gang through half closed eyes.

Carlos moved his gaze to the unassuming Sam.

"I am Sam Loes. I shall be driving the tractor and moving materials and I'll also help with the shredder. My job is to make sure that the hopper does not get empty!"

"Next."

Bagamba was a big gentle giant. He was not bright but had a barely audible beautiful bass voice. "I'm Bagamba Lalanga. I am in charge of clean up."

"Next; last but not least." He nodded at Edgar.

"Edgar Café. I'm a mechanic and have an articulated trailer licence. My job is to keep the salvage equipment running, to drive the semitrailer and to assist in the salvage as needed."

"Thank you gentlemen."

It was eerily quiet. The sun reflected off ominous clouds that rolled in toward them. Silent lightening could be seen on the horizon. It started to rain. The wind drove ice picks into the protective clothing of those on deck. Captain Jones peered through the bridge window into an ever-decreasing view. The wipers were not enough to clear the windscreen, so he turned on the rotary windshield.

The lightning was upon them and struck the foremast. With a thud the Fare Skye hit a 10-metre wave head on. The decks vibrated in recoil as if the ship had grunted following a blow to the solar plexus. The foredecks were awash and the cargo lashings strained.

It became hard to walk on deck as the ship pitched, rolled and yawed. Otto with his fragile stomach was not feeling well. His exit was not noticed. He leaned over the rail and threw up.

With a crack, sparks flew off the bow and a container fell overboard. "Mr Bjork!"

Mr Bjork was hanging on to a railing by the bridge window. "Yes sir!"

The captain took the pipe out of his mouth. "Check the turnbuckles on the containers and take someone with you. Use lifelines! That's an order!"

The storm passed. "Did we lose any containers?" Captain Jones demanded of the first mate.

His radio crackled. "Finished the inspection sir. Yes. We're missing two containers. All others are secure."

The captain scowled, took out a clipboard and pen and muttered under his breath. He found the required forms and secured them against the Masonite. "More paperwork – ugh".

Otto asked innocently, "What happens to the containers when they go overboard?" He stood up as if to look for them passing by the ship. They had long gone and were probably still afloat.

The captain zipped up his jacket. "They become one of the thousands lost each year. They usually sink, but some float because of their buoyant cargo."

The next day heralded glassy seas that seemed to lead to infinity and the rising sun promised another pleasant day. The team went outside to enjoy the vista – blue green. Ozonised humid salty air soothed their jagged nerves and was definitely preferable to Otto's smoke. Carlos watched as flying fish skipped across the wake introducing a pod of porpoises to the Fare Skye.

The wake decreased and the engines became quiet. An orange launch came towards them. The vessel pulled up next to the ship some six stories below the captain at the top of the gangway. The pilot climbed onto the penultimate step. "Permission to come aboard sir?" The pilot had a glint in his eye.

"Permission granted." He gave his buddy a pat on the back.

They had arrived.

Operation Vulture had begun.

Ming's Message

Ming dialled Manny's Milk Bar. The unmistakable voice of Li-Na brought a smile to his wizened face. "G'day baba! How are you and how is mama?"

There was a little pause. Li-Na set the phone down and looked at Manny. "She will die soon." She covered the receiver and let out a cry and then lifted the receiver to her ear. "Can I speak with her baba?"

Li-Na and Boa-Yu talked for over two hours. The phone bill was the last thing on Ming's mind.

Andrew Holmes

Monty Hindenburg had recently read a brilliant article written by Andrew Holmes, a journalist in his team. He had been eyeing Andrew as a potential international correspondent full time.

"Good morning Andrew. I have an assignment for you in Beijing to report on the war against pollution conference and then continue on to Kyiv to cover the invasion of Crimea."

He left the office to make preparations for the trip and to catch an hour of much needed sleep before the red eye flight to Beijing. He arrived in Beijing the morning of March 6th.

Bao-Yu Dies

Bao-Yu died on March 6th 2014. She took a nap at lunchtime and died in her sleep. Ming found her lying peacefully. She did not have to struggle anymore. He brought a shaky hand to his forehead; he remembered her presence, companionship, life, and energy. He wept, rather sobbed with passion from the depths of his soul.

Ming lifted the receiver and dialled Li-Na.

Li-Na answered.

Ming outlined her duties as per the Confucian principle of filial piety – 'devotion to one's parents' when she returned for the funeral.

She let out a guttural groan that morphosed into quiet tears.

She had begun to grieve.

Tullamarine

Manny called up the stairs. "It's eight o'clock and the taxi will be here soon." The front doorbell tinkled and long time friend Mohamed Moosa came in.

"All righty then. It's time to go."

Mohamed, Li-Na and Li-Li headed off to Tullamarine International Airport to start their long journey to Beijing. The Milk Bar shrank into the background as they headed off to the Melbourne airport. Li-Li held her stomach and asked about the aeroplane. Mohamed and Li-Na assured her. Li-Li was obviously more concerned about Mr Snuggles than her deceased grandmother.

The traffic was light on the Tullamarine freeway. Mohamed tried to make Li-Li feel at home asking about Mr Snuggles and her school.

They stopped at departures. Mohamed got out and fetched a trolley for the cases. He would have escorted them to the ticket counter, but the car behind honked its horn.

"Have a great flight and I shall see you at Manny's when you get back!" Mohamed drove off into the darkness.

They entered the airport, got their boarding passes and left their luggage.

They passed through security without a hitch, except the officer had to explain to Li-Li that Mr Snuggles would not be hurt going through the scanner.

She woke to the mechanical announcement: *"This will be a preboarding announcement for families with small children and those…"*

"We are on our way," she told sleepy Li-Li.

Mr Snuggles

The aeroplane was not full, so Li-Na and Li-Li had three seats to themselves on the A330-300: seats 36 E, F, and G. Li-Li giggled. "Look! Mr Snuggles has his own seat!"

"Yes. Li-Li you can put his seat belt on and yours if you can."

"Me do it mum." Li-Li tried unsuccessfully to attach the belt. A flight attendant in the economy section came over to help Li-Li. The formal bronze badge identified her as 'Jane Watts,' a flight attendant with a welcoming smile and cheery personality. "That's a lovely doll! What's your name?"

"Li-Li and this is Mr Snuggles." She held Mr Snuggles tightly afraid that Jane might take him. Sue attached her seatbelt and said that she would bring back a 'children package' once they were underway.

Jane scurried back to Li-Li with the Malaysia Airlines 'children package'. Li-Li excitedly opened the package of coloured pencils and colouring book and started to colour.

Shortly after breakfast tinny speakers announced their descent and arrival. The wide-bodied jet seemed to float over the buildings as houses grew bigger and rain streaked the cabin window. Engines relaxed for a minute as the bird floated then kissed the ground with a chirp followed by a frenzied roar that pushed passengers into their seat belts as the aeroplane slowed.

Li-Na had suppressed her latent claustrophobia. She needed to get out to decompress.

She beamed at Li- Li. "We're here angel! We're safe now."

She was wrong.

Bai Chin

Ming imagined Li-Na and Li-Li taking the first leg of their trip. He checked his watch. They would be descending to Kuala Lumpur right now.

He went to his computer, turned it on and started to surf the net. He was aimlessly following hyperlinks until he accidentally landed on a news article highlighting Manny's Milk Bar. He couldn't believe the rave review by Andrew Holmes on assignment from the Coonabarabran Times for the Melbourne newspaper 'The Age' dated 2010.

"Manny's – good old days or good old times?

"I was on my way to Alba's on Lygon Street when I noticed a busy Milk Bar with "Manny's" on the front. The place looked retro as some of the signs advertised products that have log since disappeared from the market. It has a striking blue awning but needs some external upkeep. I went inside and the same dated appearance brought me back to my childhood.

There seemed to be a group of regulars that hung around gossiping and commenting on the paper. The atmosphere was true Australiana from the Blue Hills days. One expects to see some Jackaroo from the outback appear, just to spin a yarn for the locals.

Manny's has excellent food. I recommend Avani's Indian food. Avani Gupta cooks the food fresh each day. For a milk shake ask for their Milo blast: Milo, milk and mint leaves freshly picked from their backyard.

What is so special about this place? First there's Manny a wonderful fella who makes you feel at home and sets the atmosphere. "All righty then. What will ya have today mate?" His business partner and wife is a knock down beautiful Sheila. He has time for anyone who comes in and always likes to hear a good yarn.

If you can handle 60's advertisements and enjoy good old Melbourne hospitality, then Manny's is the place.

If you go to Manny's and want more than milk, then turn off your cell phone and leave your watch behind. Go put 10 cents in the Jukebox and listen to the Beach Boys, Chiffons and other sixties singles. Manny's reminds me of the good old days.

Andrew Holmes – The Age.

Ming was surprised. He had previously thought that Li-Na had sacrificed her life for love with an underachiever. There was more to Manny than met the eye.

The men from the funeral home had taken Bao-Yu's body from the matrimonial bed. The flat was empty making the atmosphere more poignant. Ming spent the rest of the day working with Mrs Chin on funeral preparations. They consulted the Chinese Almanac for the day to hold the ceremony, hired a calligrapher for the invitations to be sent out in white envelopes.

Port Hedland

Otto had arranged for a two day docking for 'repairs' for the Fare Skye. The ship's crew were thrilled to have a day off. On March 8th.

But now things were chaotic on the Fare Skye. The crew scurried around the cargo like rats in a maze on amphetamines. The crane hook disappeared into the hold then pulled a vehicle out of the dark into the blinding light. It was red, shiny and new: one of the new mobile cranes. Ever so gently, the crane operator let down the vehicle.

Otto walked over to his employees and explained the procedure for customs and immigration. "The offices are over there at Laurentius Point. We'll go together." He knew that there would be no problems. Steve had been paid with diamonds.

They arrived at immigration and customs and waited until aisle one was free. Steve was waiting for them. He asked what they were going to do in the region until the ship's 'repairs' were completed. After platitudes about the beach, beer, weather and cars he stamped their passports and they returned to the dock.

Otto picked up a Land Rover rental. Bruce drove it leading the convoy of three road trains that had convened just outside Port Hedland.

They headed down the 138 in air-conditioned comfort.

The back was full of camping equipment that threatened to take over the front seats, Otto and Bruce were pushed forward to the dash.

Adrien drove the first crane hauling four flatbed trailers that carried shipping containers with the air compressor trailing behind.

Geraldo drove the other identical crane. It towed four flatbeds. The first two carried the excavators and the others containers. The first container held small equipment and tools for the operation. It had the generator trailing behind.

Edgar drove the blue Kenworth W900 with four trailers. The first flatbed carried the custom-made engine cradles, shredder, fuel drums and tractor. The second was empty and the remaining carried containers.

The trip to Marble Bar was uneventful. They turned right at the Marble Bar exit and then left quietly snaking down the gravel Corunna Downs - Salgash road. The convoy turned left to the airbase and lurched its way down the six kilometres to emerge onto the abandoned runways. The wrecking crew disembarked. The flies swarmed them.

They set up the temporary salvage plant.

Bagamba and Miguel unrolled the camouflage.

Edgar started the generator.

Carlos and Sam removed the small tools and Carlos wired the lighting units.

Adrien and Geraldo unloaded the excavators and tractor. The screeching of new caterpillar tracks was like fingernails scraping a blackboard.

Miguel and Bagamba unpacked the living quarters equipment. Only food and water were available. Ablutions would have to be done away from the camp.

Carlos and Sam laid out the runway lights.

Bruce took the ILS unit to the end of the north-south runway.

Miguel helped Carlos with the shredder.

Nelson examined the cradles. They had been damaged during transport. He started to cut and weld the supports back to specifications.

Bagamba had made Billy tea on the fire.

Bruce whistled through his fingers. "Smoko mates! Tea's ready!" The workers clocked off and gathered around keeping away from the fire.

"Dinner will be at 19:30."

The sun was losing its strength and so was the team. Bruce wandered around the activity ticking off jobs from a mental checklist.

The sun bled into the red sand to rest for another day. At 19:30 the men gathered around caked with sweat and the red outback dirt. They were hungry and thirsty.

Sargent Major Bruce demanded a progress report. The team reported that the Instrument Landing System was set up, lights were working, the cradles were back to specs, trailers were parked and all equipment had been tested. They were ready.

The Milky Way was brilliant making the auxiliary lighting seem superfluous especially when the waxing crescent moon struggled past the horizon. The fire had burnt down to glowing ashes supporting a Billy boiling water. Bruce took a handful of loose tea and threw it into the cauldron. Carlos was amazed when Bruce added a eucalyptus leaf. Bagamba knew the process.

Miguel looked puzzled. "Why do you put in a leaf?"

"Flavour."

"Why not use a kettle and a teapot?"

"Listen mate, when you're in the bush you use a Billy!" He lifted the handle on the open four-litre aluminium pot. "Usually, they are not as posh as this one. I get some fencing wire and a tin, emptied of course, a really big tin; you know the ones with enough spaghetti to feed 100. You make two holes in the top and the wire is the handle." The tea was boiling hard. "First you add the tea on the boil and then add a gum leaf just before spinning. Steep for as tarry as you like then swing it around your head to spin down the tea leaves." He demonstrated the process using a good underhand swing over his head gaining speed.

The temperature continued to drop while the vivid Southern Cross pointed the way south. Otto pondered the site and pointed to the stars. "It's no wonder that these stars appear on the Australian flag."

I'm Bored

Kuala Lumpur International Airport is Malaysia's main airport and one of the major airports of South East Asia. It is located approximately 45 kilometres from Kuala Lumpur city centre. It handles 70 million passengers and 1.2 million tonnes of cargo a year. The air traffic control tower is currently the tallest in the world.

Li-Na and Li-Li were tired from the overnight flight and Li-Na was concerned as to how to entertain Li-Li. She lifted Li-Li and sat her on her hip. "Li-Li how about a story. Would Mr Snuggles like to pick which one?"

Li-Li used Mr Snuggles as a puppet to pick *The Adventures of Blinky Bill*. The natural light from the large expanse of glass made Blinky Bill jump out from the page. The anthropomorphized koala smiled from the cover. Li-Na sat down with Li-Li on her knee and began to read. She was entertained for the duration of the story but when it was finished Li-Li immediately pronounced that she was bored.

Li-Na looked at the oversized red digital clock. "Only seventeen hours to go."

They were nearly there.

171

Ju Lei's Excursion

Ju Lei Wong woke early and looked up to see a dull grey sky dripping rain on the window. She slid back under her bed sheets waiting for her mother to beckon her to come for breakfast. She couldn't go back to sleep as she was too excited about her upcoming night shift observing the Air Traffic Control at Kuala Lumpur International Airport.

Her father John Wong was a senior pilot and was on a layover in Beijing before flying back to Kuala Lumpur the next day. He had been able to arrange for Ju Lei to observe air traffic control as this is the profession that he had chosen for her when she had finished her secondary school. This is not what she wanted. She really wanted to be a pilot but her father would not let her.

Li Quang Wang was the ATC (Air Traffic Control) supervisor for the evening and a good friend of John Wong. He had arranged to pick up John's daughter at eight o'clock this evening to allow time to see the airplanes and visit the working airport before his shift started at eleven.

Li Quang ushered Ju Lei to the 2011 Suzuki Swift and opened the passenger's side door. "Are you excited?" he said as he got in the driver's side. Ju Lei grinned. "We have time to look around the airport. I have a pass for you so we can go and see the airplanes up close before I start work.

172

"Let's get started. I need you to fill in these forms. You are already approved to visit many of the secure areas of the airport but you will have to be by me at all times. Do I make myself clear?" Ju Lei took a step back.

Ju Lei's response was loud. "Yes sir!"

Li-Quang introduced his student to the head of security Mr Jak Chan. He smiled. "Enjoy your evening. We may even make an air traffic controller out of you one of these days!"

The Devil is in the Details

17:00: March 7th, 2014 – Kuala Lumpur Malaysia

At 17:00 the hijack team had assembled in the Sama-Sama hotel at the airport in a boardroom that Otto had rented for the day. They were there to rehearse the night's grand larceny and to look for any possible problems that might occur during the operation.

Each introduced themselves, pilot Flavio from Angola, mercenary Brian from Angola, Tom and Sue Tong from Malaysia.

"I'm Tom and I shall be the Purser for the flight. I'm the boss of all flight attendants and have access to all cabin controls. I shall be starving the passengers of oxygen slowly before Flavio does a smoke dump to finish the job. Over to you Sue."

"I shall have an oxygen cylinder stashed in the overhead bins in business class. I'll take the coat on board as a gift for a friend in Beijing and will have GBH, the date rape drug for the pilot's coffee. The tools I require for the avionics will have been left in the electronic and equipment bay. Spare personal oxygen will also be there. Apart from that I'll bring the usual toiletries and some clothes for the desert. Flavio?"

"I'll also have an oxygen cylinder under my seat. I shall take detailed maps of the route I plan to take in my overnight bag. I'll also bring an arctic coat in a suit cover and hang it in the business class locker. I have my shorts and T-shirt for our destination."

Tom didn't have to ask Brian to speak. "I'll also have oxygen under my seat. I shall be traveling as a passenger with Flavio. I'll carry backup supplies for Sue and Flavio."

"Very good." Tom continued. I'll bring a matching kit to Sue and my coat will be wrapped identically as a gift. My oxygen will be next to Sue's."

Brian jumped in. "Flavio and I will have ours in the overhead lockers."

"Good, now let's go to the tasks." Tom looked at Flavio. "Flavio, why don't you start?"

"I'll be sitting in business class with Brian just behind the electronic and equipment access door. Tom will give the signal. I'll come forward to the cockpit help remove the drugged pilot and take over the pilot's seat. Brian will have dealt with the co-pilot. We shall be flying beyond the waypoint name IGARI and MH370 will be on autopilot. My first task will be to turn off the transponder and ACARS. Navigation lights will remain on. I shall then take the airplane up to its maximum altitude of 43,500 feet then proceed to go through the smoke dump procedure. The team must have their oxygen on at that time. I presume that before we decompress the cabin pressure will be 13,500 feet. In that case we shall need to take a lung full of oxygen every minute or less to keep alert and in good physical shape.

"The smoke dump will drop the cabin oxygen and pressure to ambient levels so the passengers will go to sleep permanently. This should not take long as their oxygen reserves will have already been depleted. You will have to let me know when I should restore cabin pressure. It will get cold inside so use your coats! During this time I shall be making a change in course, so you will feel the plane bank until we are heading west. Next I shall be making a number of altitude changes to avoid collisions and hide from primary radar. I shall have to fly the 777 manually to get past the radar and then once clear I can enable the FMS to take over as autopilot. I shall let you know when I am going to do this via the cabin public address system so you can prepare for partial weightlessness for a short time. Over to you Brian."

"My task is to help the rest of you in anyway possible. I have lots of combat experience, so if there is a problem in the passenger compartment leave it to me. We are part of an army operation; remember that! I shall also do a lot of heavy lifting with Tom and Sue."

Flavio summarised. "Next it will be pretty much plain sailing for the rest of you as I don't anticipate much in the way of turbulence, so you will have a chance to take care of business in the cabin. There might be a little shaking when I ride the jet stream but nothing of significance to your jobs. I shall contact the Corunna Downs base only twice. The first is when we have taken the airplane and passengers have been taken care of and the second when we are about 100 nautical miles off the Australian coast.

"Corunna Downs will notify me of the wind direction and speed. At that time I'll do a fuel dump and take the bird in for a final approach using as little engine power as possible to reduce noise. Finally, I'll shutdown all systems and go and help the rest of you in the cabin."

"Thanks Flavio. Good presentation. Okay. What about the avionics and other tasks?" Tom looked at Sue.

"That leaves me. I shall manage my oxygen in the same way as Tom. My first task is to greet the passengers and make sure that all pre-flight checks are completed. In other words I will be following normal procedures. I will give the captain the GBH laced coffee at this time. Basically, I'll be doing my normal job. I'll go and visit the pilots if time permits just to chat them up and see how the drug is working. I'll then ask Flavio to give me a hand with the drowsy pilot and place him in one of the toilets making sure the door displays 'occupied.' I'll then return to the cockpit and chat to the co-pilot until signoff with Kuala Lumpur. Then Brian—"

Brian interrupted. "Won't he be in the same shape as the captain?"

"No. He will not have been drugged. We need him to sign off so we don't raise suspicion. Brian, this is where you come in."

"I'll terminate the co-pilot and help with the bodies as needed."

Tom nodded and continued. "Once Flavio has the reigns, I'll join the rest of you and help out in the cabin."

"Do I have to fly with a dead co-pilot next to me?" Flavio did not relish the thought.

"Yes."

Air Traffic Control

"Li Quang. How many years have you worked in ATC in KLIA?"

"Well Ju Lei, I'm 50 now and I started in baggage when I was 19, so it's more than 30 years. Now I am the supervisor of the ATC team at Kuala Lumpur International Airport."

She looked up at Li Quang. "How many air traffic controllers are there?"

"Usually four a shift."

A man in overalls with Chen embroidered on his right chest pocket beckoned them from a white truck with a flashing amber roof light and Malaysia Airlines inscribed on its side. They drove at walking speed to the maintenance area of the airport where they stopped at a hangar.

The hangar they were in front of was immense but inadequate to hold the jet whose tailfin was exposed to the elements. "Wow!" Ju Lei's eyes grew larger. "They're big up close!"

Mr Huang, their tour guide, opened the passenger door. Li Quang and Ju Lei alighted. "Mr Wang. A pleasure to see you! I assume that this is Ju Lei, a potential recruit for an air traffic controller at KLIA's ATC?"

"Yes. Please meet Ju Lei Wong."

"Okay Mr Huang, what are you going to show us?" Li Quang noted the time was just past 21:00.

He looked down at Ju Lei. "We have a Boeing

179

777 in here for an airworthiness directive. We'll have a chance to look inside the airplane in more detail once we have seen the avionics area," Mr Huang pointed towards large steel double doors at the back of the hangar.

A nightmare of electronic components greeted them as the heavy doors closed with a slow deliberate thud behind them. A myriad of computers were scattered throughout the large room and the faint smell of burned electrical circuits permeated the stale air. Mr Huang stood by one of the workbenches. "Here is where repairs to the avionics and upgrades are made. I bet you have never seen as many computers and electronic boxes as this before Ju Lei?"

"Wow!"

"Do you know much about what computers do on a airplane?"

Ju Lei was enthusiastic. "I know that they help with directions and autopilot?"

"Correct – they do much more than that too. Computers now do the manual work, so the pilot is said to 'fly-by-wire.' Believe it or not the computers can land the airplane without a pilot! Let's go and see the computers inside the plane."

The thud of the avionics area's doors echoed around the cavernous hangar. Ju Lei appeared smaller than ever, as the tyres of the jet seemed twice her height.

They climbed the stairway into the front cabin, where Mr Huang pulled up a section of carpet attached with Velcro to a trap door.

"This is the electronic and equipment bay." Mr Huang opened the hatch. "We'll get down there to have a look, but do not touch anything! Did you know that the 777 was the first commercial aircraft designed entirely using a computer?" There was no response.

"There are multiple separate computer units and major electronic modules that control most of the plane's functions. The Data Communications Management Function (DCMF) is responsible for the communications and routing protocols for the Aircraft Communications and Reporting Service (ACARS), Automatic Dependent Surveillance – Broadcast (ADS–B), air-ground communications, and the on board fibre optic avionics network. The Flight Deck Communications Function (FDCF) implements the crew interface to the data Link function using a Cursor Control Device (CCD) and Multi-Function Display (MFD) in addition to the conventional Control and Display Unit (CDU) and printer. FDCF is also responsible for the implementation of the customer unique Aeronautical Operational Control (AOC) applications. Get it?" Mr Huang crossed his arms.

"Um…" Ju Lei was way out of her depth. "I don't understand totally. Maybe you could explain what those things are?"

"No problem Ju Lei. If you want to be an air traffic controller you will need to know many more terms like those and what they mean. Transponders, ADS-B and ACARS are necessary for you to see the aircraft at ATC."

"Why?"

"We have primary and secondary radar detection facilities. Primary detection works by sending a ping that bounces off the airplane. We see the echo on the screen. It has a limited range so we have secondary radar that sends a signal to the airplane and the airplane responds with its own signal giving back a position via the transponder, ACARS and ADS–B.

"ACARS is a system for transmitting short messages between the aircraft and ground stations via VHF radio or satellite.

"Automatic Terminal Information Service (ATIS) is a continuous broadcast of recorded aeronautical information such as weather information, which runways are active, available approaches, and any other information required by the pilots. A NOTAM is A Notice to Airmen. It alerts aircraft pilots of potential hazards along a flight route or at a location that could affect the safety of the flight."

The electronic and equipment bay could hold two or more people. "This is way cool! Look at all the lights! What's the green bottle on its side?" Ju Lei pointed to but did not touch the cylinder.

"Emergency oxygen for the pilots Ju Lei. The cabin has a different system. Lets go to the cockpit. Follow me." Mr Huang led them into the cockpit and pointed to the left seat. "Now you can pretend to be the pilot Ju Lei!"

She sat there looking around with eyes in disbelief. "Look at all the buttons and switches. How do they know what to do?"

"That's why you have to go to pilot school and then a special school to fly passenger jets. You need a license for the type of aircraft you pilot."

"So how can this airplane fly by itself?" She put her hand on the joystick.

"Well I did say it could fly and land by itself but it cannot start and take off without a pilot. It's easy. All you need to know is the direction and the elevation you want to go then dial in a new direction or altitude and press the knob. Presto the airplane does the rest!"

"How can the autopilot land the airplane?"

"It uses the Instrument Landing System or ILS. If there is an ILS beacon available the airplane can land itself following the ILS signal.

"Let's look at the engines and then landing gear."

The airplane had one engine removed for repair and it was sitting in a metal cradle. The engine looked like some science fiction space traveling device. "I didn't know it had so many pipes!" enthused Ju Lei.

"This is one of the worlds most powerful turbofan jets. In fact, Rolls Royce who makes these Trent engines can monitor them via satellite to maximize reliability and performance. So let's say engine number one has a drop in oil pressure, the sensors then send a message to the main on board computer that then sends it on to Rolls Royce via the Satellite Data Unit (SDU). Then Rolls Royce will notify the pilot to change engine load to ensure the minimum possibility of failure while in the air."

Mr Huang turned to Ju Lei who was hanging on every word. "The B-777 is built with 'multiple redundancies' as they say. Power comes from both engines and can be supplied by each engine alone should a failure occur. If both engines fail there is a backup engine drive generator with inverter. Computer failures can occur, but Boeing considered this and developed triple redundancy so that three failures would be required for a total failure. This is probably why the B-777 has the safest flying history of any commercial aeroplane."

"It must bore the pilots to tears flying one of these airplanes?" Ju Lei directed her question to Li Quang.

Li Quang mused. "I often wonder whether they're awake up there."

Ju Lei looked up at Mr Huang. "If an engine blows up and the airplane lands okay can it be replaced?"

"Yes, but there is a global shortage of these engines and no used ones."

"Thank you. I have one more question. When do the planes wear out?"

"Usually the hours in flight and number of compression cycles – take off and landing – are used to measure a plane's age. The average service life of the aeroplane in front of you is about 20 years or about 50,000 hours in flight and 75,000 pressurization cycles."

Ju Lei was gracious in her response. "Thank you. I hope that I can remember what you have shown me."

There was no time to see the undercarriage.

The arrival of the white truck was pre-empted by orange flashes reflecting off the airplane's paintwork and the sound of its horn. Ju Lei skipped over to the truck. She jumped in and gave Li Quang a high five as he closed the door behind them. It would have been faster to walk, but security rules had to be followed.

When they entered the control tower room Ju Lei could not believe her eyes. It looked as though everyone was on caffeine overload, babbling into headsets, changing plastic cards from slot to slot – moving at double speed. There were four controllers and it looked as though they could use more and this was the quieter time of day.

Li Quang took Ju Lei by the shoulders and looked at her straight in the eyes.

"Rule one: don't talk unless talked to. Pretend that you are a shadow. If you have questions write them down and ask me when I give you permission.

"Rule two: don't touch *anything* unless you have permission from me. Is that clear?"

"Yes sir." Ju Lei bit her lip.

With headsets on and in flawless English the team went about their duties.

"First there is Ground Control which is responsible for the airport areas where planes move but do not fly. These are all the taxiways, inactive runways, holding areas, de-icing and other aprons or intersections. Anyone working in these areas is required to have clearance from Ground Control.

"The next is Local Control. Pilots call it 'the Tower' or 'Tower Control.' It's responsible for the active runways. The tower clears aircraft for take off or landing, ensuring that runway separation exists at all times. We don't want any pileups! The tower might tell a landing aircraft to go-around and be re-sequenced into the landing pattern."

"Finally the Tower hands the airplane over to Clearance Delivery that gives route clearances to aircraft before they take off. This is the route that the aircraft is expected to fly after departure.

"When a airplane wants to land, we need to see all the planes to avoid a collision. We use a radar control facility referred to as Terminal Control also called Terminal Radar Approach Control or TRACON.

"I have to check on the others now, so pick a plane that you would like to follow when I get back in about five minutes." It was 12:34.

Ju Lei tried to hide a yawn. She peered into the screen and looked for a number at the bridge that matched departure times. She remembered that the first three letters indicate the airline, so she looked for her national airline Malaysia Airline System (MAS). Just as Li Quang returned Ju Lei pointed to the screen. "This one!" She had selected MAS 370 known to the public as MH370.

"Good choice. You will see the air traffic control steps of the flight until the hand over to Vietnam ATC in Ho Chi Minh City. Let's see if we can hear the ground control and the cockpit." The oversized digital clock showed 12:39 in bright red LEDs. "Put on this headset."

"I can hear them!" said Ju Lei jubilantly.

The pilot started the dialogue *Delivery MAS 370 Good Morning*

Delivery: *'MAS370 Standby and Malaysia Six is cleared to Frankfurt via AGOSA Alpha Departure six thousand feet squawk two one zero six...*

Delivery: *MAS370 request level*

MH370: *MAS370 we are ready requesting flight level three five zero to Beijing*

Delivery: *MAS370 is cleared to Beijing via PIBOS. A Departure Six Thousand Feet squawk two one five seven*

MH370: *MAS370 Beijing PIBOS A Six Thousand Squawk two one five seven, MAS 370 Thank You*

Delivery: *MAS370 Welcome over to ground*

MH370: *MAS370 Good Day.*

MH370: *MAS370 Ground. Good morning Charlie One Requesting push and start*

Ground: *MAS370 Lumpur Ground Morning Push back and start approved Runway 32 Right Exit via Sierra 4*

MH370: *MAS370 Push back and start approved 32 Right Exit via Sierra 4 POB 239 Mike Romeo Oscar*

Ground: *Copied*

MH370: *MAS370 request taxi*

Ground: *MAS37..... (garbled)... standard route. Hold short Bravo*

MH370: *MAS370 Ground, MAS370. You are unreadable. Say again*

Ground: *MAS370 taxi to holding point Alfa 11 Runway 32 Right via standard route. Hold short of Bravo*

MH370: *MAS370 Alfa 11 Standard route Hold short Bravo*

Tower: *MAS370 Tower.*

Tower: *(garbled)... Tower... (garbled)*

MH370: *1188 MAS370 Thank you*

MH370: *MAS370 Tower MAS 370 Morning*

"Ground control has passed MAS 370 onto the tower, which is where we are. I shall take the flight through the next step." He put his fingers to his lips. Li-Quang looked at the panel and flicked a switch. "We're live now." Ju Lei sat motionless listening intently. She heard Li Quang say:

Tower: *MAS370 good morning. Lumpur Tower. Holding point.. [garbled]…10 32 Right*

MH370: *MAS370 Alfa 10 MAS370*

Tower: *370 line up 32 Right Alfa 10*

MH370: *Line up 32 Right Alfa 10 MAS370*

Tower: *370 32 Right Cleared for take off. Good night*

MH370: *32 Right Cleared for take off MAS370.*

Thank you Bye

"That was easy wasn't it? Now they are going onto Lumpur approach."

MH370: *Departure Malaysian Three Seven Zero*

Approach: *Malaysian Three Seven Zero selamat pagi identified. Climb flight level one eight zero cancel SID turn right direct to IGARI*

MH370: *Okay level one eight zero direct IGARI Malaysian one err Three Seven Zero*

Approach: *Malaysian Three Seven Zero contact Lumpur Radar One Three Two Six good night*

MH370: *Night One Three Two Six Malaysian Three Seven Zero*

"Now to the radar ATC. Listen! You can follow the marker on the screen."

MH370: *Lumpur Control Malaysian Three Seven Zero*

Radar: *Malaysian Three Seven Zero Lumpur radar Good Morning climb flight level two five zero*

MH370: *Morning level two five zero Malaysian Three Seven Zero*

Radar: *Malaysian Three Seven Zero climb flight level three five zero*

MH370: *Flight level three five zero Malaysian Three Seven Zero*

"It's not too difficult when you get the hang of it," said Li-Quang. "It's never boring and a shift makes you very tired. I have not seen a serious incident since I started as a controller."

Not until tonight.

MH370 Takes Off

The aeroplane had been cleaned and the catering service was sliding the last of the food carts into the galleys when Sue entered the aeroplane. She noted its familiar smell. The pilots were settling in and beginning their pre-flight checklist.

"Good evening. I'm Rudi Jones and this is my co-pilot Dave Perkins working out of Perth and you are…" He squinted trying to read her name.

"They call me Sue."

"Welcome aboard!" Rudi looked up marking the flight checklist with his finger.

"Can I get you a coffee?"

"Bloody right!" Rudi had a hint of Swiss mixed with his Australian accent. "I'd love a coffee to keep me awake."

"Do you take it with milk and sugar?" Sue batted her eyelashes.

Rudi blushed. "Just a bit of milk but no sugar please."

"And for you sir?" She radiated towards Dave.

"Just black thanks."

Passengers in business class were boarding when Sue returned to the cockpit with the coffee. "If you want anything else please let me know. I will be in the business class section."

Dave was fixated on her. "No worries."

The passengers were lined halfway up the

walkway waiting for those with disabilities and young children to board. There was chaos and a child was bawling. Sue picked up a rag doll that she saw on the floor and pushed her way through to the child.

"Excuse me," she said politely to an apoplectic little girl. "Is this your doll?" She presented Mr Snuggles to Li-Li.

"Yeah! Mr Snuggles!" Li-Li squeezed the doll and jumped with delight.

"Now take your seat!" she said with authority. "The flight is not full so you have been assigned two seats 25D and F and seat E is free."

"That's Mr Snuggles' seat!" beamed Li-Li.

"What's your name dear?"

"I'm Li-Na and my daughter is Li-Li. We're going to my mother's funeral in Beijing. I grew up—"

Sue stopped the conversation saying, "I'm terribly sorry for your loss. I have to go back to my station now. I tell you what, once we've reached a cruising altitude, I shall come and you can tell me all about Mr Snuggles and..." she looked empathetically at Li-Na, "...about your mother. See you later!" Sue said making her way through the human shield to business class.

The flight attendants walked up and down the vacant aisles counting passengers, closing overhead bins, ensuring correct seat belt use and proper positioning of seatbacks. Tom made the announcement. *"Welcome to Malaysia Airlines flight*

370 to Beijing China. Please pay attention to this important service announcement." The TV screens flicked before synchronously providing the safety drill that few cared to watch. Li-Li was strapped in, as were Li-Na and Mr Snuggles.

"This is your captain speaking," interrupted Rudi. *"We will be traveling at 35,000 feet and have an estimated time of arrival in Beijing at six thirty in the morning local time. Please sit back relax and enjoy your flight. Flight attendants take your positions for take off."*

The aeroplane took off and Li-Li looked out the window. "I can see the lights again and wow they're getting small. It's pretty mum!"

"Yes angel, they are pretty. We'll be seeing grandbaba soon. Just one more sleep angel."

It would be a very long sleep.

Goodnight Malaysian 370

It was nearly one o'clock in the morning, but Ju Lei was not tired.

"What is a squawk?" she asked.

Li Quang picked up a large volume. "Here comes the official definition 'A discrete transponder code (often called a squawk code) is assigned by air traffic controllers to uniquely identify an aircraft. This allows easy identification of aircraft on radar.

"We'll hear the handoff to Vietnam soon."

The speaker crackled.

MH370: *Malaysian Three Seven Zero maintaining level three five zero*

Radar: *Malaysian Three Seven Zero*

MH370: *Malaysian...Three Seven Zero maintaining level three five zero*

Radar: *Malaysian Three Seven Zero*

Radar: *Malaysian Three Seven Zero contact Ho Chi Minh 120 decimal 9 Good Night*

MH370: *Good Night Malaysian Three Seven Zero*

"Now we can follow the marker on the screen."

"It's gone!" exclaimed Ju Lei."

"What the heck! I've never seen this before! Give me a moment." Li Quang sprung out of his chair. The other controllers could do little to help as they had their own planes to look after. No one had ever seen a heavy disappear before.

"As long as the airplane is flying it should show on the screen, unless their transmitters have failed."

"Does that mean it has crashed?"

"Not necessarily. If it had I would have expected a signal from the ELT – Emergency Locator Transmitter."

One of the junior controllers came over. "Ho Chi Minh City called in to say that they have not received MAS 370 and have no indication of where it is."

Malaysia Airline System flight MH370 was missing.

Hijack

Flight MH370 was flying at 35,000 feet and meal service was underway. Tom had already reduced the cabin oxygen by dropping the cabin pressure to the equivalent of 13,400 feet, a pressure just below the threshold for deployment of the oxygen masks.

Sue noticed that the air was a little thin and went to her overnight bag and took a couple of breaths of oxygen. Her sight cleared, as did her head. She noticed Flavio and Brian occasionally bent down to get some oxygen. They were seated first row of business class seats row 1 A and C just aft of the electronic and equipment bay trap door behind the galley partition. They had pink cheeks whereas the remaining passengers looked grey.

Dave called Tom to the cockpit. "Rudi seems to have fallen asleep! He was telling me about his new girlfriend and some of their antics. He's nearly 60 and unless he's bragging the woman will kill him!" Dave ran his hand through what used to be hair.

"Bloody hell! Could you take him to the toilet and splash some water on his face? He is the pilot mate!" Dave said shaking his head, glad that he was not in the same state as Rudi. He asked Tom for some water.

Tom suggested innocently. "I'll get a volunteer to help me. Do you mind me bringing someone to help into the cockpit?"

"Go ahead mate." Tom left and returned a few seconds later.

"Dave, I'd like you to meet…err…Mr Ribas who will help me."

"Call me Flavio, mate."

Rudi was heavy. Flavio's muscles had not seen such activity for years and were complaining bitterly. He needed to sit down and have a puff of life's essential element.

"Here's your water Dave. Flavio asked me whether he could sit with you for a while. He's a pilot too but flies smaller planes so maybe you guys could entertain each other through the wee hours?" Tom noted that Dave was a little slow and not as pink as he used to be.

"Great idea. It will keep me awake. I am unusually tired tonight and I have a headache," said Dave. "How's Rudi?" He jerked awake before his eyes became slits.

Tom was economical with the truth. "He's coming around."

Flavio moved into the captain's seat and put on his headset. Dave tried to break the ice. "So they tell me you fly?" asked Dave.

"Yes, but as a bush pilot. This machine is quite a lot bigger than what I am used to flying. Mind you I have had to do some wicked flying in war zones.

People shoot at anything so a smooth approach will likely get you killed."

The headsets came alive with the accented voice of Kuala Lumpur air traffic control just after one o'clock in the morning.

Radar: *Malaysian Three Seven Zero*

MH370: *Malaysian...Three Seven Zero maintaining level three five zero*, responded Dave.

"Did you ever crash or have an accident during those wild times?" Dave fought the urge to sleep.

"No but I had many one time fliers! A few wanted me to push the bird harder. I know my limits and the airframe's. It's easy to fall over them isn't it?" Flavio was working hard to keep Dave awake and unaware of the drama about to unfold. Dave looked grey and was having trouble holding his head up. A thought about Dave's loved ones bubbled up only to be drowned by the reality of his task.

"I'm twenty-nine turning thirty next month." Dave was having trouble focusing his eyes.

"We get to know each other quite well over the many hours in–"

Radar: *Malaysian Three Seven Zero contact Ho Chi Minh 120 decimal 9 Good Night* crackled the air traffic control in Kuala Lumpur.

MH370: *Good Night Malaysian Three Seven Zero*, said Dave.

Flavio nodded and Brian took his cue. Dave's young neck was no match for the mercenary's twist. Dave's lifeless body slumped forward pulling on his harness. Flavio put on his mask and inhaled deeply.

MH370 was theirs.

The Last Breath

01:22: March 8th 2014 – Near Malaysian Peninsular

Flavio turned off the transponder and the ACARS system. He turned off SATCOM, but could not disable all communications. That was up to Sue. Secondary radar could not track them now and they were mute to the world. Tom came on the intercom, "Ready when you are Flavio."

"Mummy, where's Mr Snuggles?" Li-Li was falling asleep.

"He's right next to you," slurred Li-Na.

"When will we get there?"

Li-Na slurred. "To-mo-wo-w morn…ing."

"Will grand-baba meeeet us?"

"Mmm."

"What happens … if I can't under-stand people?"

"No…" breath "…worries," said Li-Na as she went to sleep.

Li-Li leaned over and gave Mr Snuggles a hug – a long hug. She was asleep and blue.

Tom was waiting at the cabin with the intercom receiver to his ear waiting for Flavio to give the signal. *"Standby for decompression,"* crackled the earpiece.

"Ready!" he said quietly in the intercom phone and nodded to the others amongst the motionless passengers.

"I shall do a smoke dump in ten seconds." He paused for a few seconds. *"10, 9, 8,"* Everyone

made sure his or her oxygen masks were well attached. *"7, 6, 5, 4,"* All was quiet.

Even though Tom had lowered the cabin pressure to 13,400 feet, nothing could have prepared anyone for the decompression. The pain in their ears was intolerable. The passengers kept sleeping – deeper and deeper.

Li-Na and Li-Li were deeply unconscious like most of the passengers. Nobody reacted to the pressure change. As the life-giving oxygen drained from their bodies, mother and daughter were reunited with Bao-Yu. She was in a white light beckoning them to come: a place so wonderful, cosy and peaceful.

Mr Snuggles was still firmly belted into the middle seat, as were Li-Li and Li-Na in theirs. Their faces were blue. Li-Li's breathing grew shallower until she breathed no more. Li-Na was not far behind. Bao-Yu welcomed them with open arms but Mr Snuggles was not with them.

Sue gave each of the conspirators their winter coat. The coats and oxygen tanks strapped on they watched the temperature fall, 0, -10, -20, and then -30. Tom used the intercom, "Flavio? How long to go before we can close up? It's getting cold in here. Remember we are supposed to keep the bodies cool but not frozen!"

"Five minutes. Hang on!" Flavio put the flying hearse into a shallow dive. Momentary unweighting made Brian check his half full oxygen tank. Their weight returned to normal but

the nose was obviously lower than the rest of the aeroplane. Surprisingly, the engines sounded the same but quieter, the noise now coming from the air brakes.

Flavio watched the altimeter fall and checked to make sure the airspeed did not get above the airframe threshold. He gradually pulled back on the joystick and was surprised by the response – better than some single engine aircrafts he had flown, although its mass was obvious. It was a 'heavy' after all.

"Okay. Smoke dump complete. You can reset the cabin pressure and temperature." Flavio leaned forward looking for potential aircraft crossing his path.

He levelled out at 23,000 feet, a perfect altitude to recover from a non-existent stall and right between the traffic layers. "Sue. Aren't you supposed to fix something in the electronic and equipment bay?"

"Oh shit!" she said running to the trap door. She dropped down the ladder and found the toolkit. Flashing lights, noise and heat of the ventilation system met her as she groped for the light. "Found it," she said to no one in particular. She opened her book of wiring diagrams and started to work. It was more difficult than she thought to disable the SDU.

The air was becoming breathable again. *"Safe for oxygen off."* Flavio announced over the intercom into one of Tom's now deaf ears.

They had committed mass murder.

Where is MH370?

Li-Quang asked again so all could hear, "Is there any news from Ho Chi Minh about MAS 370?" The others looked blank.

He asked again. "Anything from Ho Chi Minh?" Li-Quang began shaking.

"No sir. I spoke to them less than a minute ago. MAS370 is not responding to their requests and they have no location for the airplane."

"Get Jak Chan back up here right now!"

Li-Quang filled him in on the situation. "Notify the authorities that we are missing an airplane but make sure that this is not released to the public under any circumstances! It may be a malfunction of the transponder or the airplane may have crashed."

"Okay, I'm on it."

Jak took off on the double.

The Dead

"It's now up to us to start the clean up. Remember what Sue said about *rigor mortis*. We need to get the bodies either stacked by the exits or in the aisle before they become rigid."

"Let's rock and roll," announced Flavio on the intercom as he put the aeroplane into another dive. *"This time we are going to drop like a stone!"*

The criminals hung on as they became weightless again. The change in altitude hurt their already traumatised eardrums bringing pained expressions to their faces. Tom covered both his ears while Brian tried to get his ears to pop using his little finger as a plunger. He tried to yawn. Sue put up with the pain and kept working pinning herself between the electronics racks and the green oxygen tank.

Flavio brought the aeroplane out of its dive at 5,000 feet. Gravity increased then settled back to normal. *"Is everyone okay?"* Flavio was smiling.

"I'm okay but my ears aren't," reported Brian.

Tom looked around and at the conspirators. "Let's get on with the clean up."

The cabin became cramped. There was not enough room for the bodies in the open space even when they were stacked on top of one another next to the exits. Tom had a thought. "Brian, go ask Sue for a hex ratchet with a 14 millimetre head. We need to remove some of the seats to give us room."

Brian returned with the tool. "Sue said that we should not take out the seats as they could really ruin our day if we hit turbulence or there is a hard landing. If you look at the floor you will see that the seats are on rails. We can loosen the bolts and then slide the seats together."

"That means we need to get the bodies out of the seats at the back of each section and as they're removed we slide the seat in front of them backward hard against the now empty seats. This will give better access to the next row. By the time we have collapsed all rows we should have a large space to lay out the bodies."

A large hammer and a wrench solved their problem. The seats moved.

Flavio was changing maps when Sue entered the cockpit. "Can I get you anything, Flavio?

"I'm okay. I'm busy now."

"How are you doing?"

"Trying to hide from the military radar until we're out of the straits of Malacca. That's why I am flying so low. They can only track us with primary radar and we should be out of range. I have a detector.

"You can tell the others that we are doing well and have not yet been detec–" The box screamed and flashed red furiously. "Shit d' merde! They've found us! Now we have to wait to see if they scramble their jets! I have ears on so we should be able to hear what is going on. They haven't hailed us so you guys continue and I shall handle things here."

No contact was attempted.

No fighters were scrambled.

Nothing happened.

Invisible

It was 02:00. Fa Lee had arrived at work at 23:00 yesterday. He thought about the diamonds he received from Otto as a present for his girlfriend in exchange for ignoring MH370 as it passed through Malaysian airspace. Fa Lee was the chief officer on duty and as such had control of the radar group.

The staff was tired and ready to go on break. Fa Lee looked at his watch and then the team. "It's pretty quiet so go and take your break. You all look tired and I need you on deck awake. Be back at 02:30 and bring me back some coffee." They complied eagerly with the extra break time leaving Fa Lee alone at the station.

MH370 appeared on the radar screen. He saw that it was flying low as expected. Nobody else saw the object in sovereign airspace so he logged the unknown aircraft as a so-called 'friendly.' The air force was not alerted. At 2:22 a.m. MH370 disappeared from the military radar, about 200 miles northwest of Penang up the straits of Malacca.

The team returned from their break unaware of the sighting.

MH370 vanished into the night.

Gone!

Forty-five minutes following detection by the military radar, Flavio made the decision to climb back to 35,000 feet.

Once at cruising altitude Flavio entered the route into the Flight Management Computer (FMC). In two minutes he had plotted a course to Port Hedland avoiding detection especially as most radar sites were not operational this time. Now he could take a break.

Tom did a double take when Flavio came into the cabin. "What are you doing here?"

Sue grabbed Tom. "Who's flying the aeroplane?"

"George."

Brian played dumb. "Who's George?"

"George! The autopilot" Flavio explained. "The original autopilots were nicknamed 'George' by the Royal Air Force decades ago. Most people don't use that nickname anymore."

Tom took a look at the corpses left to remove from their seats. "Okay crew, let's get the passengers out of their seats and rack 'em and stack 'em."

All the passengers were out of their seats and laid in rows by 04:00. *"About three hours until touchdown."* Crackled the speakers.

Brian started to go through the hand luggage looking for valuables and his eyes twinkled with mischief. Tom and Sue looked at each other. "Sue. We better not cross Brian. Just let him do what he wants."

"Okay Boss."

She and Tom left Brian to his pillaging.

Flavio was puzzled. What was the meaning behind the message on the screen 'Engine performance within normal parameters?' It had been on since he took over the aeroplane. "Sue? Do you know how the aeroplane knows that its engines are running normally?"

"They don't know anything but their sensors will send information to Rolls Royce!"

"I would expect a fault code if we are off line. Can you check to make sure that we are not leaving a trail? Perhaps the aeroplane is still communicating in some way?"

Sue went back into the electronics and equipment bay. "Fuck!" There was still a light on indicating that the Satellite Data Unit was still live. This was probably not a problem as they were not using communications and had turned off the transponder, ACARS and other systems. But Flavio's question had her worried. She decided to pull another module out of the rack.

There was a flash - darkness then lights again. "Phew!" Sue took a deep breath.

A new sound caught her attention. One of the backup computers was rebooting. She had to shut it down.

Looking at her wiring diagram she went to the circuit breaker board and flipped a number of switches. The culprit rack lost its lights.

"I got it!" She proudly mounted the floor of business class like an Olympic diver out of the pool and walked to the cockpit. "Sorry for the break in power. Is everything working up here Flavio?"

"Yes. The engine message centre is now giving an error message. Hopefully we are now truly invisible."

They were.

Sand Storm

The insects had stopped chirping. It was eerily still and there was not a sound except for the men chatting.

Carlos noticed. "It's awfully quiet don't you think?" They stopped talking and looked around, shrugged their shoulders and the fireside conversation continued. Bagamba did not join in because he was too shy to ask the others what they were talking about.

He looked at the stars. "Otto? Do you know why the stars are going out in the east? It should be getting lighter not darker." Otto looked at the disappearing constellations. It was as if a dark blanket was being pulled up from the horizon.

"I don't know Bagamba. I'll ask Bruce."

"What's going on in the east? Have a look at the stars." Otto pointed to the black portion of sky.

"Holy shit! That looks like a sand storm!" Sparks of lightning confirmed his diagnosis. "Everyone up and tie down anything that moves. We only have about five minutes before the sand storm hits us! Go in pairs and take a torch – GO!"

Otto had never seen a sand storm, nor had the men. The men ran to tie everything down, but

213

Otto remained seated. "Bruce. Tell me what to expect!"

"Strong winds whip up a lot of loose sand and carry it in clouds that roll across the outback like a tsunami up to 7,000 metres in height! Airborne sand blasts everything in its way. It wrecks buildings, machinery and crops. Visibility is reduced to zero."

This was something that Otto had overlooked in his plan.

Without asking, Bruce picked up Otto and flopped him over his shoulder and ran to the Land Rover. He put Otto inside. "Sorry mate. There's no time to walk!" Bruce ran off to help the others frantically tying down anything that might take flight once the stinging wall arrived.

Rarely does a sand storm give warning as to its power. This was going to be a surprise that they would never forget. A wall of dust, sand and debris hit them hard from the east. The auxiliary lighting became faint red dots.

"Protect your eyes!" The gang did not need reminding as they had their hands across their abraded faces. Sandblasted by nearly 100 kilometres per hour winds, they struggled to get to the vehicles.

The driver's door of the Land Rover opened letting in Bruce and the outback and then slammed shut. Otto turned to Bruce and dabbed his eyes. "How long before the wind drops?"

"It depends. They can stop suddenly after a few minutes, can wind down slowly or settle into a windy day. I hope they drop soon as I can't imagine the Albatross landing in this."

"Flavio can!" They sat quietly watching the seconds tick by.

Otto noticed it first. The Land Rover shook less and noise was less. "Bruce. I think it might be abating." Otto looked at the time. It was 05:49.

The rage had gone from the wind but the anger remained. The tent had blown down the runway and seven of the empty fuel drums were missing. All else was accounted for.

The wind stung at 40 kilometres per hour.

Beijing Capital International Airport

04:45: March 8th 2014 – Beijing China

Ming was excited to see his daughter after so long. He wondered what Li-Li would be like and whether she still had the doll Boa-Yu made. He got out into the acrid Beijing smog and paid the driver. Li-Na's airplane was supposed to arrive at 06:30.

It was a quiet morning at Beijing Capital International Airport. He sat in an uncomfortable chair at the end of the arrivals hall and read the paper he bought on his way in. Family members and friends congregated just outside of the customs hall for the arrival of MH370. The flight arrival information board updated and blurted out in red: DELAYED – MH370. The ETA (Estimated Time of Arrival) field was blank.

Andrew Holmes had been in Beijing since March 6th 2014 covering China's "war on pollution" presented by Premier Li Keqiang at the annual gathering of the National People's Congress. With a raincoat draped over his arm and brief case over his shoulder he dragged his luggage into the terminal.

Confused, he had gone to the arrivals area and then tried to correct his mistake in vain; linguistic difficulties sealed his fate. With less than thirty minutes until take off it was highly unlikely that he would make his flight to Kyiv to cover the Russian invasion of Crimea.

He noticed agitated people looking and pointing at the arrivals board. It displayed MH370 in red with no ETA displayed. He bumped into an old man with a Fu Manchu beard. "Excuse me sir, I'm terribly sorry! I'm Andrew Holmes reporter for Reuters. What is going on here?"

"We are all waiting for a flight MH370 from Kuala Lumpur. It is late and some are saying that it is missing."

"Missing? How can anyone lose an aircraft these days?" Andrew's eyes came to life. He smelled a story.

"Well that's the question isn't it? All these people want to know where their loved ones are. I've just lost my wife. My daughter and granddaughter were on the flight to be here for the funeral." Ming looked at his feet.

"I won't take much of your time, but if this airplane is lost I believe that you could help by giving your first hand account of what has happened." He looked up to see the arrivals board update – MH370 changed to CANCELLED.

Andrew Holmes scratched his head and looked at Ming. "Surely a flight cannot take off and then be cancelled?" Ming shrugged his shoulders.

Pandemonium engulfed the hall as those waiting began to suspect the dreadful fate that may have befallen their loved ones. At noon, the red letters announcing that MH370 had been cancelled disappeared as did the hopes of those waiting. Ming jostled to the service desk but the smiling staff had no further information.

Andrew Holmes moved away from the crowd to make a number of phone calls to cover his absence in Kyiv and find a replacement. It took some convincing Monty but he finally was cleared to report on this developing mystery.

Police collected those awaiting the arrival of MH370 into a staff area at the side of the arrivals hall. Ming was swept up with the crowd. The herd filed one-by-one into a waiting minibus bound for the Lido Hotel in downtown Beijing, a half-hour drive from the airport. Andrew Holmes was not to be left out of the action and got on the bus.

The long, agonizing wait for news had begun.

MH370 Lands

The lights of Port Hedland twinkled faintly then faded as the dawn approached. The sun was waking and stretching its sunbeams lighting clouds slightly below them in the east.

"Land Ho!" Crackled the speakers in the cabin.

Flavio announced triumphantly into his satellite phone. "Vulture base this is Albatross, over!"

"Hello Flavio." Otto's voice was unmistakable.

"We are about to start our descent."

There was a brief pause. "Be advised: strong winds from the east-northeast. Port Hedland weather shows winds 50 kilometres per hour gusting to 75 und expected to decrease during the day. Both runways are clear. Please advise your approach."

Flavio throttled back, started his descent and began to dump fuel. The aeroplane shook a little then a bump, a bump sufficient to rattle items in the galley, a bump indicative of more to come. At first he thought it was the jet stream: not so. It became obvious that there was significant turbulence and a difficult landing ahead.

The aeroplane was shaking and bucking a little now. The clatter in the galley grew louder. Flavio spoke into his microphone. *"Cabin crew prepare for arrival. Put your seatbelts on!"* The message echoed around the flying morgue.

Tom frowned and bit his lip. He looked at Sue. "Flavio this is Tom. We are still too high to be in arrival positions aren't we?"

"We'll be in for a turbulent ride and a difficult landing. You can see the red clouds. They have a sand storm down there and Vulture says to expect high winds!"

"Okay. Sue and I are belted in our seats." He reached up to return the receiver to its cradle when they hit a large pocket of turbulence. The aeroplane dropped like a cement block creating negative gravity. The receiver hit the roof. The bodies became airborne. They hit the roof then dropped to the floor.

The aircraft hit turbulence again and the bodies began to move. They became airborne a number of times gradually moving toward the rear of the cabins. Flavio noticed the weight change. *"Tom! The aeroplane is getting tail heavy what is happening back there?"*

Tom grabbed the receiver. "The turbulence is moving the bodies around!"

Flavio adjusted the autopilot. *"Stay in your seats. I have everything under control."* He was unsure that he had. The autopilot was maintaining the aeroplane's attitude but soon he would give George a break.

The phone rang. "Flavio?"

"Yes Otto."

"The ILS is at east end of east-west runway. Wind has decreased in speed to 40 kilometres per hour. Estimate the visibility is less than 200 metres."

"I will keep the line open on speaker until touchdown. There's severe turbulence at 15,000 feet. The cargo is moving and cannot be strapped down." Flavio gave the phone to Brian.

"We'll talk you down the best we can. Standby."

The aeroplane lurched in turbulence as it banked to the right. Just as he was about to finish the turn the aeroplane dropped. The bodies became airborne again. The aeroplane recovered but the bodies fell back to the floor on the right side.

Flavio had his eyes glued to the instruments. The aeroplane's attitude had changed again. The artificial horizon was not level. His leg muscles rippled under his pants as he worked the left rudder peddle and increased the right thrust. The horizon levelled. The aeroplane was flying crabwise over the Australian outback.

Flavio peered into the red cloud looking for a faint image of the ground. He turned on the landing lights. "We can send up a flare. Let me know Flavio." Otto pointed to the Land Rover and Bruce scurried off to fetch the gun and flare shells.

"Okay get them to fire a flare now."

Brian yelled into the phone. "Fire now!"

"Brian! Tell them we have ILS contact."

"We have ILS contact Otto."

"We can hear you now!" Otto said relieved. The crew jumped and waved.

Brian saw it first. "Runway straight ahead!" Flavio had sweat running down his face. He pushed the undercarriage lever down. The wind roar almost drowned out the clunk of the undercarriage locking in place and the increased drag slowed the aeroplane further.

The wind was stronger than he thought. He gave the throttles full thrust but the engines did not have time to spool up. He pulled back on the yolk. The stall warning alarm sounded ominously as other alarms sounded and the instrument panel lit up with flashing lights. Flavio ignored them.

They made the runway just missing the soft sand. The aeroplane was heavy, too low and too slow, with its attitude nose high, tail low and crablike. He could not straighten his line without dropping the right wing. The Albatross stalled onto the runway landing on its tail first, which pulled it into line. The front wheel came down with a crash. He snapped back the reverse thrusters. The Albatross roared and then rolled to a stop with about a quarter of the runway to spare.

Touch down at Corunna Downs's WWII airbase – 07:04 local time.

Flavio taxied the Albatross to its final resting place on the apron. The awaiting crew were jumping and waving their hands.

Flavio was a hero.

Welcome to Australia

Bruce and Otto looked fruitlessly through the impenetrable red cloud. The satellite phone came alive. *"We will be landing on the east-west runway from the west."*

"Scheisse! The ILS is on the other runway!" Bruce threw the statement at Carlos and Nelson. "Get the ILS to the east end of the east-west runway NOW!"

The Albatross seemed to be flying in slow motion. Then the nose lifted and it collapsed onto the runway tail first. The right main, left main and front undercarriage were next. Otto wiped his brow. "No damage to the engines."

Malaysia Airlines flight MH370 to Beijing had landed at Corunna Downs' airbase in Western Australia, miles from civilization. This was the first time since 1946 that a large aircraft had woken its sun baked runway.

Otto picked up the phone. "Congratulations Albatross. Flavio you earned your pay on that one!"

"Thanks Otto. I'm just glad that we are alive."

The camouflage was fully laid out now.

There was a sudden explosion followed by another. Tom, Sue, Brian and Flavio opened the doors without disarming them.

The explosive bolts blew out the doors and initiated the inflation of the emergency chutes.

All was ready.

Andrew Holmes Interviews Ming

Andrew Holmes was ready in the Lido Hotel lobby. He glanced at the laptop screen and read what he had written so far.

"Malaysia Airlines (MAS) issued a media statement at 07:24 Malaysian time zone (MYT), one hour after the scheduled arrival of the flight at Beijing, that contact with the flight had been lost by Malaysian ATC at 02:40 MYT. 'The government has initiated search and rescue operations,' said the MAS representative."

Ming interrupted his reading. "I think they have more news, but it is in the local dialect. Just wait a little and I shall translate what they say for you." Ming's beard was in disarray and his eyes were puffy, but he held back all visible emotion. The tin can announcement jabbered on.

Ming translated. "They say that Subang Air Traffic Control lost contact with the aircraft at 01:22 MYT and notified Malaysia Airlines at 02:40 MYT. Neither the crew nor the aircraft's on board communication systems relayed a distress signal, indication of bad weather, or technical problems before the aircraft vanished from radar screens."

"Do they have any other information?"

"They said that there's been no evidence of a crash but apparently the radar saw the missing airplane turn back before vanishing!"

"Really? Thank you very much professor."

Andrew went back to his room, opened his computer and sat looking at the blank screen, then turned on the TV. There was no new news. He brought the machine to life and sat with a blank document in front of him and then typed five words: who, what, when, where and why? He could answer all except who and why. He placed a question mark after the 'who' and sat with the cursor blinking after the word 'why'. He looked out the window and scratched his head.

Why? There must be something of value. There had been no ransom demands or anyone claiming responsibility, so political motives seemed unlikely. Cargo was his next thought. It would have to be particularly valuable cargo to warrant such a skilled operation.

He started to close his laptop when it suddenly dawned on him. The airplane was of value in itself. He bit his finger and closed his eyes. Perhaps it was taken and chopped into pieces and the valuable bits sold? He started to search the web for the value of parts of a 777. His eyes grew bigger and bigger.

The aeroplane was worth a lot.

Manny's Dilemma

Manny grabbed the receiver. "Hello. Manny's Milk Bar." Ming was on the line. He told Manny that the flight never arrived and that Li-Na and Li-Li were missing.

Manny was serious. "Flo. That was Ming. He rang to say that Li-Na and Li-Li's aeroplane is missing!"

Flo was gobsmacked. "What?"

"They never arrived and the arrivals board gives no estimated time of arrival. Ming is very upset."

On the TV, in a serious but excited tone, Mike Amor announced, *"Malaysian Airlines flight MH370 from Kuala Lumpur never arrived. It was supposed to land in Beijing at six thirty this morning. We cannot confirm the official reports at this time. Two hundred and one passengers and crew were on board. We will keep you posted as further developments occur."*

The news had one new comment. The Malaysian Military had tracked the aeroplane and they stated that apparently it turned from northeast and headed west and the transponder and ACARS were not transmitting.

Manny scratched his head. Why would someone turn off the transponder and the ACARS system? What did they want?"

With no answers, Manny looked down as the empty cavern inside him grew.

Chop Shop

Australia's Pilbara is no place for feebleness. Every day, planeloads of workers are flown in to grind out long shifts in the region's mines, amid the searing heat and red dust, for weeks at a time. It's a macho culture, where you are expected to work hard, play harder and earn big money.

The deafening screech of new caterpillar treads and the smell of diesel tainted eucalyptus smoke in the rising heat mixed with red dust and shifting sand, gave the site a post apocalyptic appearance.

Bruce's jaw muscles rippled. "Get the engines, avionics, undercarriage and then we get the flock out of here!" He covered his face and turned back to the wind.

The men dispersed. Bruce was next to Nelson. He put his hand on Nelson's shoulder and pointed to the flatbed with the engine cradles. "Nelson! Are the engine cradles ready to take the engines?"

"Yes sir!"

Sam brought the drums to Flavio and Brian. Brian stood on one of them and opened the stopcock to empty the remaining fuel from each of the tanks. They emptied the wing tanks first then the centre tank. The small amount of fuel spilt on the ground would be removed at clean up.

Sam had brought the tractor around to the tail section. He lifted the bucket so that Carlos could extricate the black boxes. Nelson was also in the bucket with the plasma cutter cutting into the tail. There was less grit in the wind at this height.

Geraldo had started his crane and lifted two rope ladders over the aeroplane: one behind the cockpit and the other in front of the tail. Bruce saw that he needed help in securing the ladders due to the fickle wind. "Bagamba and Miguel! Go help Geraldo with the ladders! I need Nelson on the fuselage now." Nelson looked at Bruce and Bruce nodded approvingly.

Edgar brought around a top-loading container to take the bodies using the Kenworth and parked it near the middle doors on the starboard side. They detached the container and flatbed then went back to attach the flatbed with the engine cradles.

Geraldo and Adrien helped Sam place the bottom of the escape chute into the container. It would have been an easy task if it were not for the wind.

It was now nearly 10:00.

Bruce yelled through his cupped hands. "I need all bodies placed in the container in less than an hour! The cabin luggage will be placed in the other container on the portside. Bodies only belong in this starboard side container."

Rigor mortis had set in so the removal process became easier. Tom was assigned with Bagamba to receive the bodies and lay them in the container.

Nelson was cutting the tail and Carlos had almost removed the black boxes.

Miguel was waiting for material to shred.

"Adrien and Geraldo. Get the cranes in place. Edgar. Bring around the engine cradles."

Bruce looked at his watch. He made a lasso motion and all gathered around in the lee of a container. "Status report!"

Tom spoke first. "All bodies have been placed in the starboard container and the hand luggage in the other."

Flavio was next. "The fuel is drained."

Sue looked at Bruce. "We have all the hardware out of the electronic and equipment bay and have removed the oxygen tank. It's a fire hazard. I suggest we empty it."

"Good. Do it. Next."

Nelson beamed "I have the tail section ready to drop and I cut through most of the nose. I shall cut the main beams in the wings and other parts of the fuselage once the engines and undercarriage have been removed."

Bruce ordered. "Edgar. Help attach the slings to the cranes and make sure the cradles are in place for removal of the right engine. Adrien and Geraldo get the cranes and slings in position. Nelson. Did you mark the lifting points?"

Nelson gave thumbs up. "Yes sir. I have marked a large X at the lifting points."

"Okay. Miguel and Bagamba help with the attachment of the slings. Edgar will join you once he has brought around the engine cradles. Once the aeroplane is lifted, Edgar will move the cradle under the engine. Nelson will cut off the mountings once the engine is lowered into the cradle.

"Once the engines are off and secured, the cranes will lower the aeroplane for undercarriage removal.

"Geraldo. Use the claw to move the materials for shredding over to the shredder. Sam will use the tractor.

"We have to remove the seats. Sue, Tom, Brian and Flavio will be responsible for the seats. Bagamba will help Nelson once the slings are attached and then help you.

Tom scratched his head. "What do we do with the seats?"

"We'll shred them." Bruce pointed to the rear of the aeroplane. "Once the tail is off, lift it out of the way and then move the shredder as close as possible to the opening. Geraldo. Use your crane."

"Sue and Carlos start stacking the avionics in the second side-opening container then assist the others wherever you can.

"Miguel. You are the key to getting us out of here fast. Keep the hopper full and if you need help let me know."

They were making good progress.

Bai Chin Helps

Ming sat on his favourite leather chair with his head in his hands, his beard poking out between his fingers. Like his beard the sky was grey. Butterflies in his stomach turned to razor blades slashing at his heart. His empty apartment amplified the void inside – Bao-Yu wasn't there.

Mrs Chin from next door brought him breakfast. "Have you heard any further news about the missing airplane?"

"No. They have not released any further details."

What happened to MH370?

Demolition

An almighty crash stopped all work. The tail let go with a sound of screaming tortured crumpling metal. The gang looked at one another, grinned and gave thumbs up.

The slings provided support for the aeroplane. Adrien and Geraldo lifted the Albatross gently while keeping the fuselage horizontal. The aeroplane swung in the wind making it impossible to line up the engines with the cradles.

Bruce looked on. "We have to stop the aeroplane moving men! Adrien and Geraldo. Leave the cranes where they are and pin the Albatross in place with the excavators while we secure the engines."

In ten minutes the aircraft was stationary. Adrien and Geraldo returned to their cranes. The trailer with the two engine cradles slowly slipped under the right engine aligning it with the rear cradle. Bruce raised his hand. "Lower the aeroplane SLOWLY until I give you the stop sign."

The engine fitted the cradle exactly and Nelson worked quickly cutting the umbilical cord. The second engine was released from its moorings without damage. The Albatross was now suspended without engines and a tail section.

Geraldo dismounted his crane walked over to,

235

and started the excavator. The claw grasped the tail and swung it around to the shredder. Nelson and Bagamba helped Edgar cut the tail into pieces using plasma and oxyacetylene cutting tools. Sam dumped the pieces in the hopper using the tractor. After a few seconds of groaning, crunching and squealing, shards of metal appeared on the conveyor belt and poured into the container.

The heat and constant sandblasting was taking a toll on the team. The men were adequately hydrated, but they had not taken in much extra salt. Bruce passed around salt and glucose tablets. "Once the seat removal is complete, you'll remove the interior. Many pieces will come off as they are only attached with Velcro. Throw the pieces out onto the pile of seats by the shredder.

The tailless aeroplane towered above Bruce and Otto. The shredder vibrated and the tortured metal screamed. Bruce looked at the height to the cargo doors and then looked at Otto. "We'll wait until the undercarriage is removed, then we lower the fuselage to the ground and then use the aeroplane's cargo crank-powered rollers to removed the cargo. Sam will take it to the shredder."

The excavators secured the aeroplane while Nelson worked in a shower of sparks underneath. The disarticulated rear undercarriage fell to the ground.

Sam and Miguel were keeping up with shredding. It was a messy job and a lot of material missed the hopper. One of the items that fell to the ground was Mr Snuggles. The wind rolled him away from the shredder into a depression in the ground. He was partly covered with sand when the excavator pressed him into the sand. Mr Snuggles was buried.

Otto tapped Bruce with his stick. "Have the bodies covered with a layer of the shredded materials! Tell Nelson to cut vent holes in the containers. Make sure they are finished by 17:00. Dismissed!"

The wind dropped and within five minutes there was no breeze. Flies swarmed them. The air cleared as if the sand storm had never existed, but the layer of red dirt on all surfaces insisted that it had.

Flavio stopped and looked around. He put his hand on his head and his jaw dropped. He was overwhelmed with the stark beauty of the outback. He felt at home even though this was the first time he had set foot on this continent. Was it just a dream?

Otto took off his hat and scratched his head and placed his hair. He looked at the details of the manifest. There was one cargo 'tank' marked 'radio parts.' "Ja. We have something that may be a bonus here – 2.4 tonnes of radio parts. Open the tank and remove them by hand."

Bruce was already in the hold. He pulled out his knife and cut into the canvass wrapping.

"Scheisse!" said Otto. "Those are not radio parts it's a whole communications satellite! Babs will be pleased."

Otto wondered about their find. What was a communications satellite doing in the hold of a commercial flight? Whose was it?

Now came the final deathblow to what was once a 261 million dollar airliner. The excavators belched and menacingly moved into the attack position. It only took 45 minutes before the sophisticated machine was in sections of scrap ready for shredding.

Flavio beat an empty pot. The gang did not take much encouragement to come for dinner. They salivated in anticipation. Little did they know that salivation is a privilege in this part of the world; it requires adequate hydration. They ate rapidly and drank their tea.

It was nearly 19:30 when they had completed the shredding. They did a walk around looking for any evidence of their dastardly deeds.

They did not find Mr Snuggles.

Without a Trace

Night brought a celestial light show with a crescent moon. The Milky Way was no less brilliant than any other night despite the storm that had passed. Everything was red from the sand storm. Otto looked and admired the work done at the demolition site.

Bruce reported that the site was clean, so Otto waved the convoy forward.

The clattering of diesels ruptured the peaceful night. The trip back to Port Hedland had begun.

MH370 would never be found.

They left the airbase with tyre tracks as the only evidence of their activities, evidence soon to be erased by the shifting sands. The convoy slipped away into the night.

Then it happened. The front left hand tyre of Adrien's vehicle exploded as it hit a pothole. They still had 10 kilometres to go before the Marble Bar - 138 junction. Bruce broke the silence. "Okay. Change the tyre. Edgar! You're in charge."

Edgar ran to the stranded vehicle. The crane was buried up to its bumper in a pothole and could not back up. They tried the jack but couldn't get it under the vehicle so they used the other crane to lift its stranded mate. The delay cost them nearly two hours.

They reached the sealed road and slipped past Marble Bar at 02:57 and reached the 138 highway back to Port Hedland.

Bruce picked up the radio. "We have three and a half hours to get to the dock. The cranes are the slowest so they go first." The convoy picked up speed and settled into a steady 90 kilometres and hour.

The road to Port Hedland was in a beautiful condition and free of traffic and animals. The Milky Way faded into a grey soon to be blue sky as the everything lightened.

They arrived at the docks at 06:33 with 25 minutes to spare. There was a lone guard by the gate waiting for them. The caravan passed through onto the dock before the trickle of unenthusiastic staff trickled in to start their day's work. The 'borrowed' equipment bound for Angola never left the ship according to the logs.

Operation Vulture was a success.

At the Wharf

Otto and the gang returned to their berths on the Fare Skye.

The group gave each other high fives and went their separate ways, except for Tom and Sue who went over to Otto concerned about their arrival in Africa. "Sue and I don't know where we are going to live in Angola."

Otto got out his coin, took a drag from his cigarette and blew a smoke ring toward Sue. "I have a house for you in the suburbs of Luanda. There will be no cost to you as long as you stay there. You are free to move, but remember Angola has no extradition agreements with your country. Don't worry; I'll make sure that all goes smoothly once we get there." He sat back and inhaled deeply scrutinising their reaction.

"Don't forget you are 'dead' und your debts have been paid. Don't shorten this opportunity for a long und happy life." Otto was deadly serious. Tom and Sue looked at each other and left the room.

Edgar ran to the deck and introduced himself to the workers stating that he had been ordered to look after securing the Angula load on the port side of the ship. The ship's crew welcomed the help. Otto had sent their boss on a one-way trip to Bali.

Edgar 'secured' the top containers with their hidden secrets. While the other stevedores were distracted, Edgar removed the locking cones from where the containers were to be clamped in place. None of the labourers noticed.

Otto looked at the weather maps on his laptop. The swirl of a tropical storm heading to north Western Australia filled the satellite view of the weather. He imagined the containers falling overboard.

The metal decking vibrated in anticipation of leaving. Tugs pulled and pushed the pregnant vessel that grudgingly left the sunburnt dock with a moan from the bumpers.

Otto looked out over the endless horizon, blew a smoke ring and poured himself another glass of Schnapps. He sat back and thought about the operation. It went well.

Babs will be pleased.

Lido Hotel

"Yes Monty. I'll be back in London tomorrow." Andrew Holmes closed his mobile.

His research had uncovered very little about the possible whereabouts of MH370. However, he had enough material to write another article.

He thought about the missing pieces as Ming moved toward him. Ming bowed and gave Andrew a photograph. Andrew looked at the picture and there was Bao-Yu with a rag doll she was making. "Please keep the photograph. I have another copy." Ming pushed the picture towards Andrew who blushed and delicately took the treasure.

He shook Ming's hand and patted him on the shoulder. "Professor. I am going to get to the bottom of this!"

He returned to his room and looked at his draft article.

Malaysia Airlines flight MH370, was scheduled to fly from the Malaysian capital, Kuala Lumpur, to Beijing in China on Saturday March 8th 2014. At about an hour into the scheduled six-hour flight it disappeared from civilian radar screen on Malaysia's east coast at about 1:40 a.m. local time. Military radar indicated that MH370 made a turn to the west at the time it lost contact with the air traffic controller. It was last detected in the Gulf of Thailand in the South China Sea.

Relatives and friends of those on board are demanding answers. Certainly, the Malaysian authorities have been less than helpful in a timely and detailed response. "I don't know how anyone can lose a large jet without knowledge of what happened," said professor Ming Goa. Professor Goa's plight is particularly poignant as his only daughter and granddaughter were coming for his wife's funeral. Like others he is alone without answers.

He checked out of the hotel and headed to the airport and wondered how the story of MH370 would finish. He bought a copy of the China daily US edition. It was gratifying to see that his colleagues had nothing more to offer than copying the articles that Reuters put on the wire.

This story might win him a second award.

Where is My Family?

The papers arrived unceremoniously with a thud at the front door of Manny's Milk Bar. The headlines of 'The Age' yelled: Terror fears over lost plane. It had rained and the temperature had dropped. Customers came in running between the drops.

Manny was counting the takings in the till wondering where his real treasures were.

Flo was wearing too much lipstick. "Any news Manny?"

Manny didn't look up. "Nah."

Later that day Manny asked Flo to look after the Milk Bar for a while. He walked aimlessly around the city.

Where were Li-Na and Li-Li?

On the Run

The Fare Skye was now in international waters above the deepest part of the Indian Ocean: the Mariana Trench. The rocking caused by the impending storm became unpleasant.

Gone were the joyful aquamarines and turquoises. Nature's palette was tinted with grey and becoming darker by the minute. The porpoises and flying fish had abandoned them as the winds increased. The sky turned jet black. In a matter of minutes, the wind and waves threatened to overwhelm the massive ship. Waves grew as the ship pitched and yawed, rose and fell, twisted and tilted through the slate grey walls of water. Visibility was non-existent as the bow sliced through the waves that crashed onto the foredeck and washed over the cargo.

"Hard starboard!" ordered the captain. With a full load, Fare Skye responded sluggishly. She was turning north to meet the rogue wave head on but didn't make it. The wave hit her broadside. As planned, the top containers of the Angula shipment broke their moorings and fell into the ocean.

Water rushed in through the holes cut in the containers by Nelson. They sank rapidly. Only one was visible by the time the ship left them behind. Li-Na and Li-Li with the passengers and shredded MH370 were now slowly drifting to a deep watery grave in the Mariana Trench some 5,000 metres below.

Time moved slowly.

Time played on their minds.

It was going to be a long trip to Africa.

~~~~~***~~~~~

Epilogue

Ming committed suicide. Manny knew that he was depressed and was devastated by his decision to end his life.

Manny became an alcoholic trying to drown the pain of his loss. Other women did not interest him and he lost interest in the Milk Bar.

Ju-Lei went on to become a pilot much to her father's chagrin.

Otto awakens nightly to his bedroom full of corpses and no amount of Schnapps can make them go away. He is alone, weak, in pain and lonely.

Babs is a lost cause. His greed shows no bounds. He was last seen in Southern Sudan 'harvesting' the oil fields. Illegal oil was turning out to be as profitable as aircraft parts.

Tom successfully completed addiction therapy and promptly returned to gambling. He is now missing.

Sue, pregnant and alone, put her PhD on hold.

Bruce settled well in Angola. The 'carrot top' was very conspicuous, so he shaved his head. He found a local girl and his first-born is on the way. Unfortunately he contracted 'sleeping sickness' and now is incapacitated.

Brian and Flavio moved to Canada. Flavio loved flying and living life on the edge so he joined Buffalo Airlines in Yellowknife, Canada, where he flew DC-3s into places more desolate than the Angolan forest. A cold snap (-40 °C), before winter began, fractured one of the cylinders in the radial engine. It failed on take off. He would have made it if it were not for the wires.

Brian took up mechanics and built an ultralite. Flavio had refused to give him lessons. Brian learned the hard way as to what a stall means.

Nathan is now spending time in Attica due to 'accounting irregularities.'

What happened to the demolition crew is uncertain. They returned to Angola and reported to Babs. They have not been heard of since.

Andrew Holmes became obsessed with Malaysia Airlines flight 370. Somehow his interaction with Ming and the others in the Lido Hotel changed him, and changed him for the better. He has now lost 25 kilos, given up the cigars, works out and runs 5K per day. His obsession with the case resulted in the dissolution of his sterile marriage. He is now a man with a mission: 'where is MH370?'

What about those who lost loved ones? Each of you has your own unique story and grief. Please may MH370 be found so that you can have closure. The authorities have not helped with your suffering. We need to know the truth and need to keep asking for answers.

For those who had persons on flight MH370, we are with you.

What really happened to MH370 and where is it? Moreover, where are the passengers? Join the discussion at www.stolen-mh370.com

About the Author

Dr. Rousseaux received his veterinary degree (BVSc) with honours from the university of Melbourne, Australia in 1977. He trained as a Veterinary Pathologist in Victoria, Australia and Saskatchewan, Canada and was the Australian-Canadian exchange recipient in 1981. Dr. Rousseaux obtained his Ph.D. from the University of Saskatchewan in 1985 in the field of toxicologic pathology. He is a Diplomate of the American Board of Toxicology (DABT), a Fellow of the Royal College of Pathologists (FRCPath), a Fellow of the International Academy of Toxicologic Pathology (FIATP) and a Fellow of the Academy of Toxicologic Sciences (FATS). Dr. Rousseaux was appointed a member of the faculty in the Department of Veterinary Pathology, Western College of Veterinary Medicine, university of Saskatchewan in 1985, from which he retired from as full professor in 1993. Dr. Rousseaux is an Adjunct Professor, Department of Pathology and Laboratory Medicine, Faculty of Medicine, University of Ottawa, Ottawa, ON; and professeur associé, Département de Biologie, Université du Québec à Montréal, QC.

Dr. Rousseaux has authored over 85 scientific publications, over 85 abstracts and is the co-editor of "Hascheck and Rousseaux's Handbook of Toxicologic Pathology" (Academic Press: 1991; 2nd Edition: 2002; 3rd Edition: 2013), a standard reference text for pathologists in industrial settings; co-editor of "Fundamentals of Toxicologic Pathology" (Academic Press: 1998; 2nd Edition: 2010), a graduate student text; and co-author of "Bioavailability in Environmental Human Health Risk Assessment" (Lewis Publishers: 1996). He has continued to practice diagnostic and research pathology. In 1992, Dr. Rousseaux was awarded the SmithKline Beecham Award for Research Excellence for his work in developmental toxicologic pathology. He has taught numerous courses at the graduate and undergraduate level encompassing subjects such as diagnostic and experimental pathology, general toxicology, teratology and experimental design. In 1996 he was symposium and program chair of the 15th Annual General Meeting of the Society of Toxicologic Pathologists "Risk Assessment and the Toxicologic Pathologist." He was President of the Society of Toxicologic Pathology (USA), a member of the Executive and Educational Standards Committees, and Chair of the Strategic Planning Committee, member of Continuing Education Committee, Annual Symposium Committee of this Society and Chair of the Investment Working Group. He was also a councilor for the International Federation of Societies of Toxicologic Pathologists.

From 1992-1999, Dr. Rousseaux was founding principal and president of GlobalTox International Consultants Inc., and was manager of the Ottawa office. He has aided in the development of regulatory documents for the Therapeutic Products Programme and Pest Management Regulatory Agency, and also has developed the basis for the data requirements currently used in the Pest Management Regulatory Agency for Category A and B submissions. He has provided expert legal support and provided standard of care assessments for cases in a number of countries. From 1998-1999, he was CEO of RSG ConsulTest Inc., an innovative integrated laboratory testing and consulting system, which he designed in 1994. He was on secondment as an executive to the Therapeutic Products Directorate and Veterinary Drug Directorate, at Health Canada and Visiting Professor at the University of Ottawa, Department of Cellular and Molecular Medicine, Faculty of Medicine from 1999-2002. Presently, Dr. Rousseaux is principal of Colin Rousseaux and Associates and is adjunct professor in the Department of Pathology and Laboratory Medicine, Faculty of Medicine, University of Ottawa, Ottawa, Ontario, Canada.

www.ingramcontent.com/pod-product-compliance
Lightning Source LLC
Chambersburg PA
CBHW020824260626
47169CB00003B/813